W9-AGE-341

ALLIGATOR
& other stories

DIMA ALZAYAT

Two Dollar Radio
Books Too loud to Ignore

Books too loud to Ignore

WHO WE ARE TWO DOLLAR RADIO is a family-run outfit dedicated to reaffirming the cultural and artistic spirit of the publishing industry. We aim to do this by presenting bold works of literary merit, each book, individually and collectively, providing a sonic progression that we believe to be too loud to ignore.

TwoDollarRadio.com

Proudly based in

Columbus

OHIO

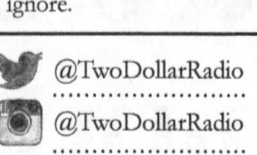 @TwoDollarRadio

@TwoDollarRadio

/TwoDollarRadio

Love the

PLANET?

So do we.

Printed on Rolland Enviro.
This paper contains 100% post-consumer fiber,
is manufactured using renewable energy - Biogas
and processed chlorine free.

Printed in Canada

100%   **PCF**   BIO GAS·   PERMANENT

All Rights Reserved COPYRIGHT→ © 2020 BY DIMA ALZAYAT

ISBN→ 9781937512897   *Library of Congress Control Number available upon request.*

Also available as an Ebook.   ***Book Club & Reader Guide*** of questions and
E-ISBN→ 9781937512903   topics for discussion is available at twodollarradio.com

SOME RECOMMENDED LOCATIONS FOR READING *ALLIGATOR* :
Pretty much anywhere because books are portable and the perfect technology!

AUTHOR PHOTO→
courtesy of the author

COVER PHOTO→
by Jared Chambers

ANYTHING ELSE? Yes. Do not copy this book—with the exception of quotes used in critical essays and reviews—without the prior written permission from the copyright holder and publisher. Without limiting the rights under copyright reserved above, no part of this publication may be reproduced, stored or introduced into a retrieval system, or transmitted, in any form or by any means.

WE MUST ALSO POINT OUT THAT THIS IS A WORK OF ***FICTION***. Any resemblances to names, characters, places, incidents, or persons living or dead are entirely coincidental or are used fictitiously.

For Alan

ALLIGATOR
& other stories

TABLE OF CONTENTS

GHUSL

Under the bright lights the skin had turned a whitish gray. A bandage wrapped around the face kept the mouth closed and flattened the black hair, made the chin thick and shapeless and pushed the cheeks toward shut lids. Rolled towels beneath the head and neck lifted the shoulders slightly from the metal bed, and under the white sheet the big toes were strung together with twine.

I will do it myself, she had said. *Haraam, haraam,* the men had replied and she had laughed inches from their faces. *And what is this? Is this not also sin?* They had waited with her for the coroner's van, had unlocked the room and shown her where the materials were kept. After they lifted and placed him on the table the eldest among them turned to her once more. *Sister, let us prepare him.* The rest shifted their eyes as she moved closer to the table, uncovered his face and asked them to leave.

Towels and sheets, white and folded, were stacked on the counter next to a plastic bucket and washcloths. She washed her hands in the sink and let the hot water run until her fingers became red and raw, the rough powdered soap granules burrowing beneath her nails. When she put the gloves on they were tight and pinched her damp skin and she pulled them off and set them on the counter. The hygiene mask stayed in its box and the incense stick stood unlit in its holder.

With a washcloth wrapped around her hand she lifted the half-filled bucket and turned toward the table where he lay. The skin to her looked coated in silver dust, like the ashes that remain after the burning of a great tree. *Up we go.* With her right hand at the nape of his neck she lifted his head and shoulders and with the left slowly and gently pressed down on his stomach, keeping cloth between fingers and skin. Several times she pressed and released, and without completely lifting the sheet wiped and cleaned between the legs in short, quick moves.

Hanna who is small

     fell

          in a well   *he got stung by wasps*

poor Hanna

          poor Hanna

            how

               did

          you

             fall?

    Again at the counter she washed her hands and cleaned the bucket. Even with her back to him she could still see his face. The thin closed lids and the brown eyes she knew had to still be beneath them. If she stood without moving she could see him sit up on the steel table and swing his legs over its edge. He would look around and catch his image in the mirror on the wall. *How funny I look, ya Zaynab.* She gripped the counter to steady herself as warm water filled the bucket.

    Where are you?

When she turned around he was still on his back, the brown eyes shut and the lips a pale violet. *Look at us playing hide and seek, even now.* She carried the bucket and a clean washcloth to the table and set them down, took her time wetting the cloth, dipping it into the bucket and squeezing it several times until there was nothing left to do but begin. She moved the sheet and looked at the hands once so small. *Give me your hand, ya Hamoud.* Cleaning now between the fingers of hands bigger than hers, moving from the smallest to the thumb.

this is Mr. Tall
and useless

this is the
labneh licker

and this is
the ring wearer

This is uncle
Abu Hatem

this is the
nit killer.

She wet the washcloth again and touched it to the forehead and slowly worked it over the eyes, the moisture clinging to thick lashes, and down the nose, her hand hesitating above the faded scar that began at the bridge and zigzagged down to the right and disappeared. He was three when he had fallen and she was nine and she had been chasing him up and down the hallway when he slipped on the black and white tiles and his giggles turned to wails. She had picked him up and held him as blood gushed from the wound between his eyes. He had clung on to her so tightly, had pulled on the skin of her neck as he cried, would not release her even when their father came running into the room.

Her eyes moved to the top of the head, the gauze that covered, concealed. *We'll clean it*, the hospital nurse had said. She had wanted to say *No*, dizzied by the thought of more hands she did not know, touching and prodding and taking. Now, her eyes fixed on the cloth until she willed them to shift, to follow instead the washcloth she ran over each arm, right and then left, flattening the small hairs against the skin. Within seconds they began to dry and she watched them shrink back into curls. She looked at the hair on her own arms, not much lighter or finer, and a smile flashed across her face and disappeared. Neither one wanting to wait for the other, they used to stand side by side at the sink to make wudu before prayer, take turns running arms beneath the faucet, carrying with cupped hands water to wet their hair and clean their mouths and noses, their necks and ears.

She waited for her breath to steady before her hand again reached toward the bandage and this time worked around it, wiping the black hair that jutted out in thick locks. Hair that once was combed back and gelled, or let loose and framed the face, played against the skin. She held her hand still and inhaled, reached the cloth's corner below the bandage and cleaned behind one ear and then the next, circled their grooves and ridges. *Even now you tickle me, ya Zaynab.* She could hear the low giggle that clambered in pitch and tumbled into a steady roll, the sounds coming closer together, the depth of the final laugh that allowed her to exhale. When she moved on to the feet, she put the cloth down and with her wet hands washed one foot at a time, reached between the toes, and massaged each sole.

The men should do this, they had insisted while waiting for the van to arrive.

And who are they to me, these men? Or to him?

Still they persisted. *You will need more people. To lift and turn and wrap.*

I have lifted him before, she had hissed. *I will remember how to do it, inshallah.*

The bucket again cleaned and re-filled, she dropped from her palm the ground lote leaves they had given her. She watched the green powder float on the water's surface. *Will you be dust now, ya Hamoud?* She stood beside the table and looked at his face. When they were children he would sometimes lie still while they took turns playing surgeon and patient and whoever moved first when poked with plastic knives or tickled with cotton swabs would lose.

Let's wash you.

Upper right side and then upper left, she knew, then bottom right and left. Head to toe. From his body the water trickled into the table's grooved perimeter, ran down to the opening that drained into a second bucket placed there. She held her breath as she loosened the bandage and paused to watch the mouth. When she saw that the lips stayed closed, a sound left her own mouth, a sigh that escaped from the floor of her chest and burst the stillness of the room. She would not lift the bandage completely, would not with her hands touch where she knew the bones would give, where tissues and nerves like sponges would sink beneath her fingers. From the cloth she squeezed enough water to wet what hair was visible, from her palm dribbled more over the back of the head. Around the neck and over the shoulder she worked the cloth, across the chest and down to the navel. When she tilted him onto his left side so she could reach his back she was surprised at his weight and felt the muscles in her arms strain to keep him from slipping.

The last time she had picked him up he was ten and came only to her shoulders in height. Their father had not come home from work and their mother sat in the kitchen whispering into the telephone in between splintered sobs and breaths that dissolved in the cold air. She had found her brother on the living-room carpet, shaking. He had wet his pants and a silent panic had pinned him to the floor, would not let his body do anything but tremble like the final leaf on a winter tree. She hoisted him up, her arm around his waist, and asked him to walk. But his legs continued to quaver and she knew then he could not stand. In one move she lifted him and wrapped her arms around his legs. In the bathroom she undressed him and sat him in the bathtub, and only when she made the deep low sounds of a freight ship and splashed her hands like fish pirouetting out of the water did the shaking stop.

Keeping the sheet over his torso she reached beneath it, cloth wrapped around her fingers, and cleaned underneath and between the legs again, down the right leg to the toes and then the left. Thoughts of unknown hands that might have touched where she now did, their intentions different and beyond the things she knew, she forced from her mind. A strangeness remained in their place. She knew she would have to repeat it all. Three times, five times, nine. *Until you smell like the seventh heaven, like Sidrat al-Muntaha itself.* But with each repetition, her movements became less certain, and she glanced several times at the face in reminder as she wiped.

When she filled the bucket one last time, the colorless camphor dissolved in the water and released a smell that reminded her of mothballs and eucalyptus, of rosemary and berries. She removed the sheet still covering him and left only the small cloth spread from navel to knees. In the fluorescent light his bared body looked long and broad, and she thought of once-smaller hands she had cupped in hers, narrower shoulders she had held. From head to feet she poured the water and inhaled the scent that rose as it ran along the table's gutter and splashed inside the plastic bucket.

I saw a butterfly with my eyes
                        flitting
           it was   around
                   me

                       I ran trying to catch it, but it   escaped
           from my hands.

                   Where is the butterfly?

                          It flew

                                                                away.

She unfolded one of the large towels and began to dry him. Gently she lifted his head, dried his hair one lock at a time, felt the water soak through the cotton and onto her hands. The skin of her fingertips had shriveled from so much water. *They might never dry again, ya Hamoud.*

The day they returned her father, with clenched fists her mother had beaten her own chest, pulled handfuls of hair from her scalp until the neighbors came. Her brother screamed for doctors until someone pulled him away. She was old enough to know that no doctors were needed, that what now lay in the courtyard, covered in burns and cuts and skin that curled back to reveal shredded muscle and blood clotted and congealed, was a body she no longer knew.

She stepped back and looked at the body before her now, clean and damp. She scanned for places she had missed, where she might again pour the water and run the cloth. At the sound of the door opening behind her she moved closer to the table before turning to see the same older man from before, the only one who had spoken to her. A younger man followed and between them they wheeled another table, smaller and without grooves. She stepped aside and stood silent as they positioned it next to where he lay, but when the younger one began to unfold the stacked shrouds, she drew closer, placed her hand on his and made it still. With eyes wide he pulled his hand away and stepped back, but when he opened his mouth to speak, the older man leaned toward him and whispered words that kept him quiet. *Wallah, they don't know what to make of this, ya Zaynab.* She could hear the amused tone, the smile in the voice.

Two large sheets she unwrapped and placed, one atop the other, on the empty table. The smaller sheet she carried to where he lay and unfolded over his body as they watched. Her hands hesitated when the sheet reached his neck and she could not lift all of him at once, she knew. She drew back enough to allow the men to move to either side of her, her fists tightening at her sides when with gloved hands they reached for him. As they lifted him the neck gave way and the head tilted back and she pressed her feet to the concrete floor. After they lowered him onto the second table and the head again rested flat, the older man reached beneath the sheet and removed the cloth covering the thighs. The younger man gripped the sheet's corners and began to pull it higher. She moved toward him. Stood close enough to feel the youthful swell of his belly protrude and recede with each breath, to make out the nose hairs that shivered as he drew air. Again the older man intervened, held the younger by the elbow and led him toward the door.

With the soil still new on her father's grave, they had come for her brother. Men with masked faces and heavy boots who slapped her grandfather across the face and threatened to tear off her clothes as her mother watched. *And like a good boy you sat so quietly.* In the kitchen cupboard behind pots and jars and sacks of rice and flour. When they left they took her grandfather with them, and the blood drops from her mother's nose spread like petals on the tiles.

She stood now at the counter mixing the sandalwood paste in a small bowl. Over and over she inhaled the scent and tried to keep her hands steady. *You will smell like the earth, ya Hamoud, like a tree and its soil.* Back where he lay, his face still uncovered, with her fingers she dabbed the paste onto his forehead and nose and rubbed it in, but still the brown tinted his pale skin. With his hand in hers she worked the paste into one palm and then the next, reached beneath the sheet and dabbed the knees, and then the feet. She wished it were her feet on the table, her legs, her body. Imagined his hands stained brown as he touched her forehead instead. But his face, as she imagined it, contorted in silent grief, pushed the thought from her mind.

The three of them had arrived in a new country seeking darkness, the quiet of unlit rooms and the absence of knocks. A place where names had no meaning. Together they searched for the missing pieces of their mother, the stories that had shed their words. Not knowing why, she felt relief when he grew taller and bigger than she was. When he was found in the early morning hours behind the shop where he worked, his skull opened and spilling blood that ran through the black hair and onto the asphalt, she had been the one to call for doctors.

I had a little bird.

    I looked after him,

        and when his feathers grew and he was big,
        he started to peck my cheeks

            Zik zik zik zik zeek

Gently now she bent the left arm so that the palm flattened against the chest, folded the right arm so that the right palm rested on the left. *And this is how we pray, ya Hamoud.* When he was six, she had taught him to bend and clasp his knees with his hands, to touch his forehead to the ground. Her parents laughed that he was too young, but she had spent years waiting for him to grow, to learn words and what they meant, so that she could show him things, teach him what she knew; the alphabet and how to ride a bike, the names of animals alive and extinct, the planets in the solar system and their moons. So when she stood beside him on the prayer rug and told him to move as she did, he did as he was told, touching hands to chest and then to knees, forehead touching the carpet and back up again. For years after he would only pray if she led.

She stood beneath the bright lights, her fingertips grazing the sheet's edge. Her eyes traced the arc of his brows, the hairs that strayed from their place. She imagined what they looked like when he smiled, the way they drew together, and noticed for the first time the thin lines near his eyes. *Whose eyes will see us now?* Her mother, she knew, would never speak again. Her own words as she pulled the sheet above the mouth and then higher still were like boats with neither sails nor oars. After the sheets were wrapped around him, the center looped with ropes, the ends fastened, she stood with empty hands. *Make me like a sandwich, ya Zaynab.* She would have him lie on the bedsheet and roll him from one end to the other, and through the layers she could hear his giggles. If her mother or father was walking by, they laughed with them. *Make sure he can breathe, ya Zaynab.*

DAUGHTERS OF MANĀT

She woke to the same slight wind drifting through the drapes. Again the early dawn shadows spread across the ceiling, gray forms that appeared to be reflections of other shadows, a mirrored image from time primordial, its source erased. Outside, the ensemble of birds grew louder. A quavering tangle of notes. Who else do they wake?

In the bathroom she brushed her teeth, combed her hair, and in the mirror saw only the outline of her face. With the lights off she dressed, a long dark skirt and a light blouse, thick tights and high boots. She passed a makeup brush across her cheeks and with her moistened fingertips smoothed her brows. The sound of her heels on the stone floor crushed the birds' chorus, and when for a moment she stopped moving, only a single warbler's interlude reached her ears. A thin melody that trilled and rattled. She walked to the window and opened the drapes, lifted the pane. Stepped onto the windowsill and jumped.

As she fell her skirt unfurled and blossomed, and those who saw her from beneath said she glided across the sky. Her body blocked the rising sun but her sheer blouse absorbed the early rays so that she glowed. A baker opening his shop watched her beam brighter as she moved, until she was an orb ablaze, a burning Venus. A pastor on his way to the day's first service paused in the street to cross himself and plead the precious blood of Jesus. The Lord of Phosphorus was again in their midst.

She felt as she fell that time had slowed. Before her the earth spread indefinitely and though she knew she hovered high above the ground it seemed to her that there was but one plane and that it contained land and sky alike. This flattening allowed her to see far beyond her street, her city. She could make out the curve of Africa's horn and the blue of the Red Sea. What else did she see? A Simien fox hunting a mole rat, a masked butterflyfish searching for its mate. She realized the earth was smaller than she had been led to believe, that only its curvature had made its parts seem discrete.

**

By the time she was twelve, my aunt Zaynab was taller than her father in stature and fuller than her mother in shape. Her hair was black and bright and reached down to her waist. Her lids were rimmed in double rows of lashes, a genetic mutation that made her eyes gleam like polished sunstone. Boys she had grown up with, neighbors' children, who used to tackle her to the ground in games of tag and give her piggyback rides up and down the narrow, hilly streets of East Amman, now moved out of her way with quiet reverence, with mild hostility.

After months of turning away suitors who stood at the front door with sweaty palms gripping boxes of sweets, and chasing away others who trailed their daughter home from school and hissed at her heels, my grandparents decided something had to be done. Zaynab herself had learned to not mind the stares and catcalls. She had a quick wit and a serrated tongue that could raze the confidence of even the most cavalier suitor and to her the boys were more like feral cats, skittish and afraid. But, as they say, it was a different time, and girls like that had to be looked after in measured ways. And so by age twelve, my aunt was married.

The man was in his twenties and came from a devout family that agreed to my grandmother's demand that Zaynab remain chaste until she reached womanhood. The first time I heard Zaynab's story I wondered how they could tell. Would it be when she grew taller? Was that how I, too, would become a woman? My own mother was shorter than some children. Was she not one?

Child or not, Zaynab was put to work in her in-laws' home, sweeping the courtyard and scrubbing the tiles, pulling hair clots from drains and chopping onions for soups. Crates of onions, pyramids of onions. So many that even in her old age my aunt despised them, would cover her nose with her sleeve, curse the day she was born and rush outside to escape their smell.

I don't know how long young Zaynab had to endure her husband's family – my grandmother would say two weeks, Zaynab claimed two months – but every day at sunset my aunt would escape her in-laws and return to her family. Each night she stayed later and later in her parents' house, cursing both families and bemoaning her fate, crying hot tears and spitting at the floor, promising misfortune for them all. Each night she was dragged back to her new home, her hair wild and voice hoarse.

When the neighbors intervened, it was with prayers and support, teas and ointments, but nothing worked. Zaynab remained ferocious, going so far as to cut off her black, bright hair – so short that the tops of her ears protruded. 'Like a boy elf!' my grandmother would say. Zaynab threatened to do more, to take to the streets and humiliate them, to scream their names to strangers. Finally it was agreed that a mistake had been made, and to everyone's relief, the marriage was annulled.

**

My aunt Zaynab looked after me while my parents were at work. She was seventeen years older than my mother and her own children were grown and gone by the time I came along. I spent more time with her than I did with anyone else and for years I thought this meant I was destined to become as ugly as she was. Arthritis gnarled her fingers into claws and too much bleach made her scalp look like parched earth. 'You think it matters how shapely your mouth is, how long your nails are?' she would say to me, leaning in close enough for me to taste her cigarette breath.

On my tenth birthday she made white cupcakes frosted purple and dropped them off at my school after lunch. As she stood in the classroom doorway holding the tray, she peered around the teacher to find me, her squinted eyes darting among the rows of children. I gave her a quick look of thanks and turned away, hoping no one would see her. That afternoon we had a classroom party and wore pointed hats. Beneath colorful streamers and floating balloons my friend Oni kissed me on the mouth in between bites of cake. Disney songs played from a small cassette player on the teacher's desk and the teacher, Ms. Nolan, was busy showing a student how to properly take Harry the hamster out of his cage, how to hold him with cupped hands so he felt safe.

Licking frosting off my lips, I giggled at Oni, who smeared more frosting on her mouth and leaned in to kiss me again, but within inches of my face she was snapped back by Ms. Nolan's hands and led outside. I put down my cupcake and looked around at the other kids. I wondered if they had been watching us. What had they seen? Some of them crowded near the window, pushing and pulling one another to get a look. Through the glass I watched Ms. Nolan's mouth move rapidly as she spoke and Oni's lips tremble like she might cry.

A sudden scream caused us to turn away from the window to see the kid who had been holding Harry chasing the hamster across the room. Soon, more than two dozen students were on the hunt, trying to catch Harry and put him back in his cage. But the hamster was frightened and wouldn't stop scurrying, kept weaving his way between backpacks and books, desk legs and human ones. It wasn't long before laughter gave way to shrieks. Papers flew through the air and kids tripped over one another in pursuit. By the time Ms. Nolan heard the racket and rushed back inside, it was too late. Someone had stepped on Harry and one of his beady black eyes had popped from its socket, dangled at the end of a thin bloodied nerve and stared at the carpet.

**

You wake, stale smoke clinging to your tongue, whiskey rising from your skin. The first few drinks of water scrape like sediment against your throat and you force yourself to swallow. At the bathroom sink you scrub smeared liner from your lids but a faded gray rims your eyes, impervious to soap and water, insisting on its permanence. You brush your teeth and gargle and brush a second time as you turn on the coffee maker in the kitchen. When you comb your hair, the finest strands come loose from their follicles and fall. After five, ten, fifteen years on your head, they become invisible when they reach the carpet beneath your feet. What else do you shed unaware?

Between sips of coffee you squeeze beige paste from a tube and rub it into your skin until even freckles disappear. The mascara is dry and clumps between your lashes, and you hold its wand beneath a trickling faucet for a second, two, and push it back into the tube, give it a shake and again twist it open. Count to five strokes per eye. When you run lipstick across your lips you feel their dryness, the creases where the color will gather and form thread-like veins of red. You button a blouse and as you pull on a pair of tights, you notice a run in one of the legs. The skirt, despite its length, cannot cover it. When you open the window a fly buzzes past your ear and over your shoulder. Perfectly still it perches on the dresser, facing you, its eyes examining you.

As you fall you wonder what you will sound like on the asphalt, if your face will look like those in movies, wide-eyed in surprise. You hope the bleeding is mostly internal so no one will become sick at the sight. Moments pass before you realize the fall has slowed, that you are adrift in the air and that while you cannot control where you go, you may turn in any direction you like. You feel your eyes changing, pushing against their sockets as each becomes a thousand eyes, and though they no longer move, they see all things, millions of images converging to one.

That is when you see them, standing side by side. The eldest among them is garbed in black and the second glows like the sun. Only the youngest draws near, hands you one of two swords she holds and whispers in your ear. What does she say? She asks why you have stopped calling her from the rooftop in worship, why your children no longer bear her name. You tell her you have neither rooftop nor children and that you never learned to pray. You try to follow her, to float as she does, but again you begin to fall.

**

When I was seventeen I had sex for the first time in the laundry room of my boyfriend's house. His parents were in the kitchen making dinner and we were supposed to be in the family room listening to music and studying for a physics midterm. Instead the music's volume was turned low so we could hear approaching feet as we reached for each other beneath the open textbooks on our laps. He had leaned over and kissed my neck, his fingers reaching farther down, and though we'd touched each other before, it was the first time it felt fervent, nearly urgent.

Aside from the washer and dryer the room had shelves of cleaning products and mops and brooms that hung from hooks. I wrapped my fingers around his neck and kissed his mouth, and again I felt the same rise and swell inside me as I pulled down my pants and then his. He let out a small laugh and I did too and we kissed again to silence our nerves. For the first few minutes our movements were careful and cautious as we fumbled with each other's bodies and tried to quiet our breaths.

When finally we got going, pushing against one another in that small space, I felt my body birth desire and fulfill it, felt this to be significant and myself significant with it despite where I was. The room was hot and we were sweaty and my body began to slip from his hands. But he tightened his grip and hoisted me higher and held me closer. 'You're so fucking pretty,' he said and he pushed himself deeper inside me. 'You're so fucking pretty,' he said again and I felt his arms grow strong against mine.

**

Zaynab's second marriage was to a man with clear blue eyes and a dark mustache. Though he had a large belly and limbs like meatless chicken bones it was agreed he was a handsome man. During her engagement party, she changed outfits a half-dozen times, in and out of dresses beaded and sequined, pumps and sandals high-heeled and shiny. Her husband clasped strands of pearls around her neck and slid thick gold bangles over her wrists. By then she was nineteen and even more beautiful than before. The envy of every girl in the neighborhood, my grandmother said. Those who were not invited crowded around the windows to catch sight of her, to watch how she styled her hair for each dress, how her eyes glowed bright yellow.

Still she remained as brazen as ever, smoking cigarettes and drinking beers with her new husband and his friends well into the night. Her dresses grew shorter and her hips wider and everyone who saw her offered warning. 'The smoking will make your skin sallow,' they said. 'So much beer will make you gain weight.' She sent them off with jokes and stories, pinching the fat of their arms and pulling on the skin that sagged from their faces. But at my grandmother's insistence she began to wear an amulet, a sapphire eye that hung from a chain around her neck and rested in the space between her breasts.

When, after five years of marriage, she still could not conceive, everyone agreed there was no one to blame but those who had envied her, had quietly cursed her health and beauty for so long. My grandmother took her to healers, to soothsayers and sheikhs, and finally, to the best fertility clinics in Europe. It would take my aunt Zaynab another five years to get pregnant and give birth to my cousin, Reem. It would take only three months after that for her to walk in on her husband in bed with another woman, his bulbous belly bouncing atop her behind.

Here the story gets murky. Soon after discovering her husband's infidelity, Zaynab lost control of the left side of her face. Her eyelid drooped and even when she slept, remained ajar. Half of her mouth sagged so she could no longer smile. My grandmother said a stroke had caused the paralysis. My mother thought it was shock. After all, how could Zaynab bear the news that the woman was not only her husband's lover, but also his second wife and mother to his other three children?

**

In my first year of college a guy my roommate had gone on four dates with punched her so that her eye turned black and her nose bled. At a party the night before, a friend of his had seen her kissing someone else, and the next evening he waited for her in the hallway of our apartment building to ask if it was true. As she unlocked our door, she admitted that it was. She began to apologize when she felt his knuckles bash into her face, continued to feel them across her body. 'I fucking liked you,' he said several times as he hit her.

I came home from class to find her on our living-room floor, folded over, her face covered in blood. I had never imagined her tall body could look so small. She had bruises on her arms and neck, spit in her hair. At the hospital she was admitted and treated and then inter-viewed by two social workers, a therapist, and three cops. With one eye bandaged she looked at each of them directly, with her mouth swollen nearly shut she repeated her answers. When they left my eyes wandered to her naked feet, the chipped red polish she had the night before complained she didn't have time to fix.

The guy was arrested and bailed out in under an hour. His hearing was set for three weeks later, and in the courthouse I sat and listened to my roommate give the same answers and repeat them while staring at the person that had drawn blood from her body. I listened as the judge sentenced that person to a year of counseling and six months of community service after a tepid exchange with the prosecutor and the defense attorney about what to call his crime. Had he inflicted serious bodily injury? What were the benchmarks of injury? Was it a matter of simple or aggravated battery? Domestic battery demanded an intimate relationship. What constituted intimacy?

**

It will feel heavier today, the rising. Our bodies' weight will suffocate us, press upon our shoulders and lungs and make it difficult to breathe. We will want to stay in bed, to lift the covers above our heads and let our lungs heave in silence. To imagine a slate that wipes black to gray and gray to white will help us move. In the bathroom mirror, we will see your face, not ours. Your eyes like veiled opals, your brows like question marks. Where do you roost? From where do you watch?

When the coffee boils, we will pour it and drink at once so it scalds our tongues. Our knuckles will ache and we will rub them in apology. We will remember how our fingers clutched at playground bars and how we were strong enough to catapult our bodies through the air, to land on tanbark whose splinters were incidental to the miracle of flight. We are older now, we will say. There are wrinkles, delicate but discernible. Skin thinner and less even. The makeup does not hide it and instead we will cover our marks with clothing. Cotton and wool and silk that know how to do what we still don't. We will wrap a scarf around our necks and tighten it until we feel veins throbbing and pulse slowing, and release. When we open the window cold air will hit our faces and we will lean against the windowsill and inhale. We will try to forget that the air we breathe is not ours.

Outside we will walk the length of the street while staring at the sidewalk. A dime-sized egg speckled violet just fallen from its nest and cracked, its yolk spilling onto the asphalt, will have us looking for signs of life. A black eye; an unformed beak. We will feel exhausted, reach for mental lists of who does what where and resist the urge to lie beside the broken shell in mourning. Instead with newspaper we will pick it up and place it at the foot of the fenced-in tree. Dust to dust, life to mud. The warbling in the branches will be low-pitched and hoarse, and it will quaver in our ears for hours.

The day will pass and the light will become dark. From the window we will watch the crescent moon cradle the sun before both disappear. That is when we will call to you with our loudest voice. You are black stone and white granite but are you not also our mothers? By the salt, by the fire, why have you forsaken us? Again we will hear only silence.

**

When I shaved my head my grandmother refused to speak to me. 'Tell her she looks like a boy,' she said to my father when I came home to visit. All weekend she walked around the house with her beads in hand, muttering spells and prayers and shaking her head. 'Tell her she will never find a husband with her hair like a boy,' she said.

I was about to graduate college and two months pregnant. My friend Alex drove me to the clinic twice in one week. The first time, the nurse spread a cool gel on my stomach and moved the ultrasound wand in circles. She directed my face to the screen, but I was already looking at the gray mass moving there. She began to explain the image, its fuzzy sections and barely visible parts, and if she saw my eyelids close she pretended she hadn't. On the second visit, the doctor was an ugly woman who put me to sleep and performed the procedure. When I woke up, she said kind words and held my hand.

'Maybe now was not a good time to look so hostile, no?' my college counselor suggested when he saw my shaved head. I was going on as many job interviews as I could, determined to not move back home after graduation. It wasn't until my sixth interview that a receptionist called me back to her desk after I had met with the office manager. 'This might not be my place but maybe you should think about wearing a wig, just until you're done with treatment or until it grows back. I'm just trying to be helpful. It makes people pretty uncomfortable to see others that way.'

At the graduation ceremony my parents' smiles beamed from the audience when I was introduced as the class speaker, and I could hear their claps above all others when I finished my speech. At the reception a professor told them how proud they should be and lauded them for raising a strong daughter. My father assured him that he was more than proud, that I had proven myself as worthy as any person. 'Man or woman,' he added. My mother smiled and nodded, and turned to me as the professor walked away. 'So many good things ahead,' she said. 'Thank God your hair is growing back.'

**

Eventually Zaynab's face returned to normal. She had spent the worst of those days crying, my mother said. Moans slow and long like some ancient call. But it was not long before she became placid, speaking only when necessary, unable to draw together enough energy even for her infant daughter. It was only when she regained control of her facial muscles, when she could smile and grimace at will, that she seemed to re-ignite. If she was biting before, she was now caustic. If her jokes had been improper, they were now vulgar.

She was not allowed to divorce her husband, not that she had wanted to. Instead she smeared the name of his second wife to any and all willing listeners, of which there were many. At him she hurled every insult, from sunup to sundown, until he ceased to come home. When relatives visiting from other towns would ask where he was, a content smirk would stretch across her face as she answered. 'Oh, he works a lot. Works late into the night, really. May God bless his loins.' Or, 'Who? Oh! Is that the impish man on the nightly shows?' People were aghast, my grandmother said, or pretended to be anyway. They knew the stories and they all claimed to know the truth. They demanded that Zaynab be the one to answer.

So when Zaynab began to spend her free time in the corner shop chatting with its owner, a man known for his throaty laugh and dirty jokes, no one voiced an objection. Not because they approved, but because they did not dare. Only my grandmother tried to reason with her. 'What will people say?' she begged. 'You have a daughter to consider. Who will want to marry someone with a loose mother?'

One day Zaynab packed a suitcase and my then three-year-old cousin and without telling friend or family, neighbor or stranger, eloped with the man from the corner shop. 'Maybe now people will stop talking,' my grandmother said, her face wet from wailing. 'Don't be silly,' my grandfather said. 'They'll talk even from their graves.' After six months in the U.S., my aunt Zaynab gave birth to a second daughter, my cousin Farah. And then every other year for the ten years she was married, she gave birth to one more.

**

I have been moving now for five years. At times I stayed in places long enough to memorize where the shadows fell at dawn, to learn which birds sang in the trees. But eventually I left. For three months I dug foundations and mixed concrete in one place. For a full year I planted seedlings and watered the plants that grew from them. I learned to weave chairs from bamboo, to build protective barriers around turtle nests and runways so the hatchlings could find their way to the ocean without getting lost. In all this time, I have not gone home. On the phone my mother's voice has grown colder, my father no longer asks when I will come back. Only my aunt Zaynab laughs at the sound of my voice.

When her third and final husband died, Zaynab refused to mourn. My grandmother, older and widowed by then, did not interfere. Even when Zaynab was seen laughing in public, wearing yellow and violet, her hair newly bleached and permed, my grandmother shook her open palms at those who spoke. 'Enough,' she said. 'Words have a taste, just like food.'

A month before I had left I'd swallowed fist-fuls of pills and at the hospital they pumped my stomach twice to get them out. I had taken them while in bed, had pulled the covers above my head and closed my eyes. Falling asleep I had seen a lionfish swimming among the cor-als, a koala perched on a eucalyptus tree. The air was clear, and I could breathe. I woke up in a hospital room filled with the smell of disin-fectant and the sound of my parents' screams. They yelled at doctors, at nurses, at me. 'Please get better,' they said. 'Please make her better.' As everyone else moved about the room in fevered frenzy, only my grandmother stood still, rubbing my feet with one hand and work-ing her beads with the other. 'Listen,' she said. 'Hundreds of female names in our language, but ours means triumph and nothing else.'

When she died two years ago I sat near a drying river thousands of miles from home and tried to imagine what she was like as a girl. I had seen only a single photo from before she was married; already by then her eyes were those of a woman, an island in rolling ocean. She had been married at fifteen, had borne seven children before she was twenty-four. With her hands she had sorted a lifetime of rice and lentils, had gutted fish and deboned chicken. She knew how to upholster furniture and help grapevine spread and climb, how to cover bruises and scars so no one could see them, how to measure the value of her life and still rise.

They sleep, and in shadowed lands unsheathe
their swords and thrust them at who comes.
False warriors swathed in robes try to crush
them with their stones, stab them with their
daggers. But the morning star appears, flushes
the sky a milky pearl and lights their way. The
blood they draw is soiled but feeds the land.
Clusters of acacia trees sprout and grow at their
feet, their flowers shade them as the day grows
hot. Three cranes, with black-tipped wings and
bright red crowns, circle above them, exalted
monarchs of their skies.

When they wake it is in gardens, labyrinthine
and immense. Thick walls of boxwood keep
them from seeing in any direction and they are
not tall enough to peer over the edges. Instead
they call to one another through the plants, follow each other's footsteps as they fade. Though
the road is sinuous, eventually they find its end,
a sheer cliff's edge that beckons them to fall.
They retreat, some quicker than others, some
lingering near the tip, considering the weight-
lessness of their bodies if they fall, the weight
of them if they stay.

It is only when the first one tilts over, seem-
ingly stumbles into air, that more approach.
One by one now they jump, some with eyes
closed and legs pulled up toward thumping
chests; others with arms spread and flapping,
voices echoing as they go. Some dive, headfirst,

arms at their sides, bodies like arrows. At different speeds they descend, some directly down like raindrops, others more slowly, in smooth, undulating motion as if across invisible hills.

What do they see? A gazelle nursing a lion, a camel running through a valley, its face unbridled, its back unfettered, the air damp, clear.

DISAPPEARANCE

The summer Etan Patz disappeared, New York was burning something fierce. 'It's hotter than a hooker in hell,' my father would say after a day's work, his collar slack and soiled, his scalp like wet sandpaper.

For three months our mothers kept us indoors, wouldn't let us out no-way-no-how, convinced that the man who'd snatched Etan was prowling the neighborhood for more. I imagined a lunatic in a sorcerer's cap stirring a pot of boys with a broom handle, bending over and pinching their thighs to feel for tenderness. Wondered what we'd smell like in that pot. Probably something awful, all that Kool-Aid and Play-Doh, gym socks and rusted pennies, pooled together like that.

'Let me out, woman,' I'd demand each morning and duck in time to miss my mother's palm swinging toward the back of my head. I hated her in those moments, my larger-than-life warden, wide and rubbery like an inflatable raft sheathed in floral cloth. Why I had to be kept from the swimming pool, baseball games and sugar cones balancing scoops of rainbow sherbet, I didn't understand. She never budged, not once. Stayed like that too, the rest of her life, unyielding as a nail in cement, until we buried her. Even then, at the very end, she'd still go on about 'Poor Etan.'

Only thing that kept me from grabbing a bedsheet and parachuting out the window that summer was Tommy Palansky. He'd moved into the apartment beneath ours and his mother wasn't letting him out either. We'd spend every morning running up and down the stairs of our four-story building, the light filtering in through window panes thick with dust and falling across us in streaks of gray. We'd gather Legos, rubber balls, wadded newspaper, candles melted down to their stubs, old slippers – anything we could filch undetected. Then we'd position ourselves on the steps on either side of the stairwell and build military posts out of broken-down cardboard boxes and plastic tubs and declare War with our ragtag arsenal. My brother Ralph would stand in the doorway and watch, drooling all over himself and saying nothing.

'Ben, let Ralph play with you,' my mother would holler from the living room where she sat peeling potatoes or snipping green beans into a colander, the record player behind her always screeching nothing but Fairuz.

'All he does is drool, Ma,' I'd yell back. I'd hold real still then, listening for the creak of wooden baseboards beneath her swollen feet. Sometimes she'd leave me be a little longer but eventually she'd come, her weight pressing down on linoleum and thudding across the cement of the stairwell. She'd pinch my ear between fingers, plump and damp, and pull me so close I could make out the short black prickles sprouting from her chin.

'His whole life people gonna look to us to see how they oughta treat him,' she'd say. But the kid really did drool everywhere, spit that mixed and mingled with all the other fluids he leaked. Sweat and snot and saliva on his face and neck, t-shirts, every Tonka truck and green army man we owned. The heat made it worse. He'd wake up dry enough and by lunchtime he was like a sponge left in a bucket of dirty water.

Rubbing my ear, I'd take his hand and lead him to my post, prop him up on the front line and hand him artillery to launch at Tommy. He was good at taking orders from me when he was in the mood for it, I had to give him that. Would strike Tommy on the shoulder with empty shampoo bottles and right on the head with wooden blocks.

'That's not fair, there's two of you now,' Tommy would groan. 'Pipe down. He's like half a damn person,' I'd say. Then Tommy would get bored and start crawling on all fours, hooting and roaring and pounding his chest like a mad gorilla or some other wild beast. He'd circle Ralph like that, coming close enough to sniff him and then retracting in disgust. Guess I couldn't blame him. The kid smelled like pickled eggs most days. Ralph never would react. He'd just stare right ahead and you couldn't be certain if he was actually seeing Tommy or even looking at him. I can't say I felt bad for my brother then the way my mother did. Didn't see any sense in feeling bad for someone who didn't seem to mind.

'What do you think he thinks about?' Tommy asked. I couldn't guess what went through Ralph's mind any more than I could name what was broken in the first place. I was three when he was born and my mother would say I spent a couple of years just waiting for him to get up and play. I'd try giving him my newest Hot Wheel, my best Transformer, even tucked a pillowcase into the back of his collar so we could make like superheroes and fly. But he never had a want for any of that. Sure enough he got up and learned some words but his eyes, they just didn't move like ours. It was like we were nothing more than stagehands to him and he was waiting for the show to start.

By noon the stairwell would get too hot to bear and we'd escape to the basement, where walls of exposed brick escaped the sun's reach and remained cool to the touch. Except for a few empty trunks and a lone chair there was nothing much else in the space. Sometimes our mothers would let us carry down a couple of fans and we'd set them up near opposing walls and position Ralph in the center. Then we'd veer and tilt around him like jet planes, spreading our arms and letting the breeze make its way through our thin t-shirts, drying our underarms and sending shivers down our spines.

Spent, we'd collapse onto the floor and talk about our dwindling summer in captivity and the approaching start of another nine months spent in classrooms that smelled like mildew and vinegar. 'Is he ever gonna go to school?' Tommy asked once about Ralph. I didn't answer. My father had wanted Ralph to go to school, even tried enrolling him in special classes for a few weeks the year before. Then some kid scratched him up pretty bad, pressed a pencil with a broken tip into the soft flesh of his wrist and dragged it up and down his forearm until the skin broke. All that afternoon Ralph said nothing about it. Sat through the rest of his classes and dinner, even watched some *Tom and Jerry* with me. It wasn't until she undressed him for a bath that my mother saw the carved skin, the dried blood flaking off like red ash. That's when she put her foot down and said No more. She got approval to home-school him then, but not before she clomped down the stairs and the three blocks to the school and made every official cower or cry.

Without fail our basement conversations would soon turn to Poor Etan. Whole afternoons we spent imagining what happened to him. Six years old, same as Ralph, and he goes missing the first time he walks alone to the bus stop. How's that for luck? We imagined him holed in a basement like ours, tied up and invisible to the world. Sometimes we'd really get into it and invent entire scenarios. We imagined him stoned to death and buried alive. Burned in a fire as an offering to some cult god, his screams growing in pitch as the flames surged upward. We imagined him skinned and hanging in one of the meat shops in Chinatown, like a rabbit waiting to be fried or baked for dinner. I could always picture it so perfectly. His photo was on the news each night and on the cover of my father's paper each morning. I knew his face better than I knew anyone else's, maybe even my own. Hair blond and long like a girl's. Eyes wide-set and blue. A smile that cut into his cheeks and spread past his lips, a smirk to maybe say it was all a joke, that at any moment he'd reappear.

Sometimes we'd bring down some twine and take turns tying each other to the chair and pretend that one of us was Etan and the other the kidnapper. Ralph'd just drool and watch. Our weapons of combat would transform into torture devices and we'd pretend to slit each other's throats and ply fingers off one by one while yelling things like, 'Gimme all your dough,' and, 'Where's the cash stash, punk?' We knew a kidnapper wasn't gonna ask for money – but we couldn't quite figure what it was he would ask for, what it would be he was after, so we carried on like that. My mother found us once, after I'd tied Tommy good and tight to the chair and was threatening to zap him from here to Jupiter with my plastic gun if he didn't tell me where he'd hidden the goods. She nearly tore us to crumbs but my father, who was just getting home and in no mood for a fight, said, 'Salwa, they're like caged ferrets. You gotta let them have a tumble every now and again.' Still, she told Tommy's mother and made me carry the fan upstairs. But by the end of that week we were back down there and at it again.

When we were feeling really daring we'd creep down to the ground floor, a small open space that housed abandoned bicycles and the door to the outside. I'd drag Ralph along so he couldn't tell on us and Tommy would twist the metal latch and pull the door, thick and hulking, and we would stick our heads out one by one into the humid air. Soon enough we began daring each other to step out onto the pavement, to walk to the corner where the Guatemalan man sold fresh fruit and cigarettes, and eventually, to sprint full speed around the entire block once if not twice. Even now, more than thirty years later, I can remember the way the warm air filled me as I ran, how it surged and swirled in my lungs. I must have passed the fruit stand then and taken a right, ran past Earl's Drugs and Stuff and the video store, turned right again and rushed past Didi's Donuts, the hotdog cart and the laundromat. That must have happened but I couldn't tell you at the time what I was passing, the streets feeling new and foreign even though I'd walked them all the years of my life, had known nothing but their shapes and colors. Instead, I glimpsed the curves of lips and angles of noses, the arches of brows and lines of grimaces. A bald man with a diamond ear stud leaned on a shuttered shop, a suit in a fedora brushed my arm as he passed, another wearing nothing but shorts and sneakers bounced a basketball as he went. I ran fast enough so I didn't look at any one of them directly, couldn't tell you the colors of their eyes, but knew that they could look toward me, could see me if they wanted. As I rounded the final corner, I'd erupt into something of a frenzy, a current coursing through my veins, leaving me feeling at once fearless, like I could do anything, and relieved that I wouldn't because someone was expecting me to return.

I can't say exactly when it was that Ralph went missing. I just know it was the week before we started school and the sun was low enough to turn everything orange.

Tommy's parents had gone to visit a relative in Queens and my mother had offered to watch him until after dinner. I never invited my school friends home in those days and a sleepover was unthinkable. The one time I did have someone over, this kid Joey, Ralph drooled all over the Chinese checkers Joey'd brought with him and during dinner, kept his mouth clamped tight while my mother tried to feed him steamed carrots and rice. By the end of the meal, his face was covered in orange pulp and Joey was staring at him like he was a zoo exhibit. The next day the entire class was talking about it.

Sure, Tommy wasn't especially keen on Ralph always hanging around, but he knew Ralph, knew what being his brother meant and didn't mean, what it said and didn't say. When I found out Tommy would be eating with us, I begged my mother to cook something normal. It was 1979 and exotic-sounding dishes with names like South Sea Beef and Chicken Tahitian were all the rage – culinary experiments that ended with my father sweating just trying to keep them down and Ralph spitting half-chewed chunks onto his plate until she caved and made him a hotdog.

That night though, she'd agreed to Spaghetti Bolognese and the smell of crushed garlic and simmering tomato sauce wafted down to Tommy and me as we stood on the ground level of the building, bent over with hands on knees, panting. We'd already run around the block three times each while Ralph sat and played with his plastic trucks.

'Come on, Ben. Just let him go once,' Tommy said, still gasping for air.

'Why?'

'Because I'm bored just doing the same old thing.'

I shrugged. 'We could play Legos.'

'Oh, come on. He wants to go, don't you, Ralph?' Tommy looked to Ralph who had picked up a truck that was down to its last wheel, was flicking the wheel with his finger to make it spin.

'It's almost dinnertime,' I said. 'Anyway, he won't do it.'

'Sure he will, he'll do anything you say if you're the one to say it.'

Ralph glanced up to me just then and I remember searching for something in that look, for a twitch or a well-timed blink. Anything. But on it went, that endless gaping stare.

'See?' Tommy said. 'He's just waiting for you to say it.'

I stood there for what must have been no more than a minute but it felt like all of time was stretched before me, pulled like Silly Putty in all directions at once. My ears burned and I knew my face would follow. I remember wishing he would just say something, that he'd open his mouth and a 'Yes' or 'No' would make its way out of his garbled brain. I'd heard him speak before, knew he could. But the one time I needed him to, he couldn't. Wouldn't. Instead he sat silent and watching and I felt my insides grow hot, like someone had lit a match in my stomach and left it.

'Fine,' I said. 'Ralph, run around the block one time.' Tommy let out a small yelp and pulled open the heavy door. Ralph slowly rose and walked toward it, never breaking my gaze as he moved. I hoped then that he would just turn around and run up the stairs instead, decide to watch television or cling to my mother's skirt as she cooked, anything. See, I'd say, I told you he wouldn't do it.

But he did. He walked through the door and took the five steps down to the sidewalk, squinting his eyes to adjust to the light. And then I knew it was actually happening, that Ralph was gonna run around the block alone, be outside alone for the first time, and I just wanted it to be over. 'Run fast, Ralph. Around the block, okay?' I called. 'Just fast and around the block.' But he was no longer looking at me, had turned his eyes to sky and sidewalk.

He had just taken off toward the fruit stand, his arms stiff at his sides but his stride certain in its direction, when I heard my mother bellow my name from upstairs. Tommy shook his head, signaling me to ignore her. But again she called, louder this time and I knew she'd come barreling down those stairs, her legs thick and bowed like a charging bull's, if I didn't answer. I stood in the doorway and called to Ralph, but already he was at the corner and had escaped the reach of my voice. Again, my name left my mother's lips and echoed in my ears. Tommy was now pushing me toward the stairs, knowing we'd both be punished something awful if we were found out.

I took the steps two at a time and found her bent over the television. 'I wanna move it to the kitchen, Ben. Tired of all this walking back and forth.' If she had looked at my face for even an instant she would've known right then and there what I'd done but she was struggling to get a firm hold of the thing. 'Come on, try to get the other side.' It was heavy, that television, the kind built into a wooden console as if it didn't have a right to exist alone, had to be disguised as a piece of familiar furniture first. It was too cumbersome to pick up but impossible to push.

Our difference in size didn't help either. Even after getting it up, we had to put it down and re-lift every few steps. The sweat stood on her brow and her dress clung to her like cling film. I would've felt sorry for her if I wasn't so worried about the trouble I'd be in if she knew. While we took a break to catch our breaths she asked after Ralph and I told her he was on the stairs with Tommy. I pretended I knew that for certain. Wanted to believe I knew that for certain. Enough time had passed.

When we'd finally moved the damn thing into the kitchen, just as she raised her head and turned her eyes to meet mine, I made for the door. 'Fetch Ralph and Tommy and come back up here. That's enough for one day.' I left without answering, nearly fell twice running, slipped and slid down the last few stairs. When I got to the ground floor, the big door was shut. I stood there a moment, confused, even turned around and looked back at the staircase, somehow expecting to find Tommy and Ralph standing there, waiting. But I was alone.

I pulled open the door and though I'd not been gone all of maybe fifteen minutes, already the light was changing – the way it seems to grow brighter right before it turns purple and disappears altogether. To my right a couple stood, arguing. The man was calling the woman names that to this day I don't like to repeat and she was swinging at him as he cursed. The man started to turn toward me so I glanced past him toward the fruit stand where a mother paid for a bag of mango slices for her daughter, lit a cigarette for herself. I turned my head in the other direction but aside from a mangy cat rummaging through the trash, the sidewalk was empty. Taxis and cars honked at one another on the street, their headlights coming on pair by pair as the light faded. My chest felt tight and flat, like the whole of the sky was pressing down on it, like I was no more than God's rolling board.

I stepped out onto the pavement and heard the door slam behind me before I realized that I had no way back in without buzzing my mother. The arguing couple were walking away now and the mother and daughter were crossing the street. I scanned the sidewalk in both directions two, three times and just started running toward the stand, rounded the corner and picked up speed. Everywhere I looked, my eyes sought Ralph, tried to remember what color shirt he was wearing, whether it was blue or green, the one with Batman or the Joker. I began to feel faint and sick like when you eat too much or not enough, like I was full and empty all at the same time.

I ran until I realized I'd circled the block three times and each time I saw new faces and the same faces but with something new about them. A scarred cheek, crooked teeth, sunburned skin. I looked them directly in the eyes, searched for some clue as to where Tommy and Ralph had gone, of who had seen them, who had taken them.

On my fourth time around, the fruit vendor had started to pack up his goods and nodded to me as I passed. With each step I took, what light remained seemed to scatter even faster, eager to leave the world or at least my part of it, and I became less afraid of what my mother would do to me and more frightened for Ralph and what the sorcerer would do to him. I remember wishing that something big would happen, like a tornado or an earthquake, just so it would be bigger than what was happening then. The only thought that kept me from screaming right there on the sidewalk was that I had to keep running. That, and I knew Tommy had to be with him, that Tommy would follow that sorcerer to his dungeon and save Ralph, and Etan too. He'd free them and tie up the sorcerer in their place.

Thirty minutes later, I sat on the kitchen floor, huddled in a corner while police officers went in and out of the apartment, their radios buzzing with codes only they understood. My father had gone out with a search group scouring the neighborhood on foot. Tommy's parents had returned; his mother stood in the hallway outside our apartment screaming at the cops to go find her son while his father sat in our kitchen with his head in his hands.

Over and over the same police officer kept asking me to repeat the story, how I'd left Tommy and Ralph on the ground floor, that maybe we had opened the door to let in air, that maybe we had taken turns going outside for just a few minutes at a time. The questions kept coming – the same ones with the words rearranged, until my mother turned to the officer and said Stop. But even then she wouldn't look me in the eye. That's how I remember my mother to this day, though she'd live another twenty years before dying from too many cigarettes. She kept pressing the thumb of one hand into the palm of the other, pressed so hard I thought she'd push a hole right through. She stopped only to hold up a picture of Ralph the cops had asked to see. 'No, he's not blond. It was the light in the photo studio. Made everything look different,' she kept repeating.

Neighbors showed up in turn at our door offering to pray with us and though I never knew my mother to miss a Sunday mass, she told them they'd be more useful walking the streets, searching. But I prayed anyway. Jumbled together Hail Marys and Our Fathers, promised to give Ralph my toys, to never want another thing again if only he'd appear. At some point, a cop asked me to come down to the landing, to show him exactly where we were playing, to describe who stood where and when. I looked to my mother and though she nodded, still her eyes refused mine.

A few cops stood on the ground level of the building, the door now wide open. I could make out a news truck and reporters, more cops and neighbors. A woman in a red blazer noticed me then and rushed toward the building. The cops quickly filled the doorway and stood between us. Still, I could see her peering over their shoulders as others joined her – a mass of shifting microphones and cameras and voices. The officers ordered them to step away from the door and pulled me back but not before I heard one of them ask if I'd witnessed the disappearance.

When the cops found Ralph tied up in the basement, my mother let out a cry so loud and terrible, a long howl that waned into a low moan. They walked in on Tommy holding the plastic gun and Ralph's head welted where Tommy'd struck him with it. Ralph sat shirtless in that chair, his arms and legs bound, his *Fantastic Four* tee gagging his mouth. Dried tears ran in streaks down his neck and his pants were soaked, the stench of piss filling the room. When the cops led him through the door of our apartment and into my mother's arms, he turned to me for no more than an instant and though his eyes neither twitched nor blinked, I understood them.

I don't know what became of Tommy. His parents moved out the next day and the apartment stayed empty for months. That night, my mother bathed Ralph for nearly an hour while my father stood in the doorway and watched over them both without speaking. I sat in the hallway, waiting, until my father turned to me and said it was time for bed.

I lay in the darkness and looked across at Ralph's bed, wondered what Etan's bed looked like, empty like that, night after night. I waited for what felt like hours and crept out of bed and down the hallway. My parents' bedroom door was open and I could see my father asleep in his work shirt. In the kitchen, the spaghetti sat on the table, untouched. I found my mother in the living room, Ralph wrapped in a towel and asleep on her lap. I sat next to her and for a long time I couldn't be sure if she was awake or asleep, her breaths low and far in between, her eyes difficult to see in the darkness. Then, at around dawn, when the shadows in the room began to shift and I could make out her face and she could make out mine, she pulled me toward her.

ONLY THOSE WHO
STRUGGLE SUCCEED

It was the night of the office Christmas party and Lina felt lucky
and excited to be included as she was merely an intern, although
there had been allusions to, if not promises of, a permanent position in the new year. Because she lived an hour's drive away, and
because she had to go into the office the day of the party, there
was the question of how she would get ready for the outing. Her
roommate reminded her that a gym membership they shared,
a gift to the roommate from parents who found the roommate's
weight bothersome, was the solution to her dilemma. So, after
a day of reading scripts and writing notes that summarized their
strengths and weaknesses, going on coffee runs and picking up
lunches, Lina said, 'See you later,' to her co-workers, and went
to the closest gym to which the membership allowed her access
and made use of its showers and changing room. She blow-
dried her hair straight and carefully flat-ironed and sprayed the
fine hairs that framed her forehead and which she knew would
otherwise frizz and curl in the party venue's humid indoor air. It
was a nervous energy that filled her as she applied her makeup,
and she recognized it as one of anticipation, the same she had
felt several times before. To her it signaled that her ambitions
and desires, to secure for herself a role in the company and
gain acceptance into an industry that was derided in public and
celebrated in private for being discriminatory and exacting, were
ones she could access and with time obtain. She felt in that
moment the very potential of her life revealed. Before leaving
the locker-room she looked at herself in the mirror a final time,

felt satisfied with the pale gold shadow that brightened her eyes, and wiped off the red lipstick she had previously thought festive but which now she deemed made her lips appear too prominent and defined.

The party was held in a bar closed to the public for the occasion, and when she entered her co-workers were glad to see her, and she spoke to men and women who in the office spoke only to one another or to their own assistants. As she made her way around the room, she was welcomed into the various intimate groups that formed, reshuffled and formed again, and was included as gossip was exchanged about people whom she did not know, but whose names she recognized enough to allow her to join in on the laughter that ensued at their expense. Such interactions, she understood, were the blocks required to build relationships which, if they were carefully maintained, could later act as bridges capable of delivering her to the most coveted positions. As she conversed and laughed she began to feel encouraged that the months she had committed to working without pay, complying with requests and orders that were at times intended to humble or diminish her, were in fact worthwhile, and that she was, at last, to be admitted into a life that had initially seemed too extraordinary for someone like her to achieve. She stood near the bar and accepted the drinks handed to her, and later, when the president of the company, for whom she interned directly, and the vice president, who had flown in from New York and stayed for the party, gathered a select few and handed out shots of tequila, she found herself full of verve and jubilance, feelings the gathering evidently inspired within those comprising the small group around her. And thus, though she preferred vodka to tequila, in fact found the latter sickening, she drank it, and then another.

Speaking to a second intern, who was much newer than she was and had been included in the small group taking shots near the bar, Lina learned the girl was completing her last year at a highly esteemed private women's college on the East Coast. This intern, though polite, did not smile much, and it made Lina aware of the ache in her own cheeks from smiling and laughing widely through the night, and she allowed her face to relax. When the company president sat beside her and the other intern, and discovered where the latter attended college, and where she had been raised, Lina did her best to convey interest and engage in the conversation even though they spoke of a world whose distance from hers made it mystifying and at times unreal. As they spoke, she worried that perhaps this connection, between the president and the intern, would threaten her own chances at a permanent position, and would make inconsequential the time she had devoted. Her education at a public university, well ranked, but public nonetheless, and large, and which before that moment had been for her the greatest accomplishment of her life, seemed now crude when measured against the finely tailored education of the girl sitting beside her.

When she began to feel drunk, she did not worry. She had, earlier that week, made arrangements to sleep at the apartment of the president's assistant and his girlfriend following the party. Though she did not particularly like the assistant, as he was selfish and crude, she had with time developed a reluctant fondness for him on account of his dedicated, if compulsive, work ethic, which made him resourceful and energetic, and imbued him with a sense of humor. She also liked that he thought her smart, smarter than the other interns, and trusted her to read scripts other interns were not allowed to see. With time, his trust of her had come to serve his needs primarily, she knew, as she would often be left to cover his desk on his days off and sent scripts to read and provide feedback on in the middle of the night. He told her he would, of course, take credit for some of the work she completed, but that on occasion, when it mattered, and to the president directly, he would credit some of her work to her. He promised also, in return, to help her secure a job, either at the company or elsewhere once she graduated. She had learned, both in college and in previous internships, that this was an industry that operated in such a manner, was not put off by this knowledge, and had in fact been spurred to seek a career within it partly due to its demand and difficulty. Growing up with little money, she believed, had prepared her to work long hours and to live frugally, and she had, on several occasions, felt irked by those people whom she encountered at the various jobs she held in college, in clothing shops and call centers and deli counters, who seemed assured of something large and yet-unknown in her path, as there had been in theirs, and which would keep her from realizing her goals. Their worries and complaints were, she repeated to herself, imagined and self-imposed and particular to them, and, in this way, she remained steadfast in her commitment to succeed.

When the other intern excused herself and left Lina and the company president alone, Lina felt comfortable enough to make a joke and was relieved when he laughed. She had been working for him for five months and though she found him intimidating, it was because of how he carried himself with poise that was notable and rare. Only on occasion, when someone, usually his assistant, made an error that led to his appearing uninformed, did the president raise his voice. This was different, she knew, from the men who owned the company, and the many others like them, who screamed often, and insulted the people who worked below them, and were known to resort to physical violence from time to time. The president, in contrast, was not boorish and had about him an air that was calm and regal. She was happy to speak with him and was happier still when he thanked her for her work, and complimented her on her good taste in film, and inquired about her goals and the career she would like to one day have. They spoke also of family, she keeping to herself that what worried hers most was money, and he sharing with her his struggles to connect with teenagers who, to him, seemed to overnight become different people than the ones they had been as children. After some time, he thanked her for being easy to converse with, and admitted these were not subjects he normally spoke of in such depth. She, in return, complimented him for setting a good example to the people who worked beneath him, and for being measured and kind, especially to the interns. He was taken aback by her words, but she could see he enjoyed them, and he confided in her that his years of focused work had, yes, brought him much success, but at the great price of two failed marriages and a feeling of loneliness he found difficult to describe.

These things Lina would, the next day, remember, but what occurred after was to be captured and recaptured in frames by her mind as it attempted to place in order events she would absorb as random and discrete. They would include the president offering her one of his children's empty beds for the night; the vice president telling her the assistant had disappeared after a fight with his girlfriend; the lights dimming; the vice president assuring her she would receive a room at the hotel; the bar closing and her gathering her belongings; the vice president ushering her into the backseat of a chauffeured sedan; the room spinning; the assistant telling her the plan had changed, that he and his girlfriend could no longer host her as planned; the voices slurring; the vice president informing the president that the company had, for the use of employees, reserved rooms at a nearby hotel, whose name she recognized as one located on a well-known boulevard; the faces blurring; the assistant instructing her to get into the car.

When Lina woke and found the vice president on her she wondered if maybe she was imagining him there. There, on her face and neck and hips and thighs, and 'No,' she said, and he stopped. Then he was on her again, and the room spun, and she spun with it. His tongue felt like other tongues and she thought *maybe*, then thought about the tongues she had in the past known and wanted and the distance between such tongues and this one was too vast, and the inability to calculate it overwhelmed her. What was occurring she felt was a sequence of awakenings in which first she noted how the room spun and she with it, followed by him, there, and there. Then, the unnerving feeling of this sequence being one of many, and that somewhere in the room they were stacking, amassing to something that could soon be summed and made whole. Her need to make it stop and him with it brimmed and receded, brimmed and receded, as she woke and slept, and the room spun. Her hope was for the waking to last long enough to flood her, to expel from within her the dismay and dread that kept her soundless, and when finally it did, she saw that her waking, and the awareness that came with it, would in fact be quick to saturate her through and through, and she cried, loud and plenty. This brought the movement above her to a stop, and at last she could feel him not on her and heard him walk away.

In the morning, she was calm though lightheaded, and she thought that perhaps he was gone and she could rise and gather her things and leave undetected. Instead, he came into the room and sat next to where her legs stretched beneath the covers, and said he had been drunk and so had she, that he had slept on the sofa on the other side of the door, that he was certain nothing complete had occurred, and 'I'm sorry.' He told her also that her car had, the night before, at her request, been brought from the party's venue to the hotel, and on the bedside table placed the ticket that would allow her to collect it. She did not tell him that this was a fact she did not recall, and remained silent as he said some other things about how if there was ever anything he could do to help her, she should not hesitate to ask. She noticed then the business card he held in his hand and watched him lean toward the bedside table and lift a pen, and on the card write a number he informed her was his cellphone. 'Just in case,' he said as he stood up. Then he kissed her cheek and left. The relief was immediate, and she turned her attention to putting her things back into her shoulder bag, and, on reflex, walked the length and width of the suite and its rooms in search of anything that might testify to her being there. She was beginning to sense the complications to her reputation and career that her presence in the suite could cause and was meticulous in her search. Finding nothing, she decided it was okay to leave. Before she did she looked out of the window and imagined someone like her, or actually her on a previous day, looking up at the window of that expensive hotel on that well-known boulevard and imagining that the people who stayed there surely led lives full of liberty and ease.

The valet took her ticket with a smile and she hesitated to ask for it to be charged to the room and to give *his* name, but she could guess the cost to park in such a place, and so she did. When her car pulled up to the curb beside her, its dented side and back bumper sent the normal rush of embarrassment through her. Though, in that instance, her shame was met with a degree of relief at the car's familiarity, and this shift in feeling softened the interaction between her and the valet, her handing him, as a tip, a five-dollar bill he might have guessed she could not easily afford, and her smiling in gratitude at his stepping aside to allow her to get into the driver's seat. When the door closed, it quieted the sound of the street, and she breathed the car's damp and dust, and felt the seat that after so many years had molded its shape to her back. On the freeway she was thankful the day was a Saturday, with neither classes nor her having to go into the office, with him, for his leaving Los Angeles and returning to the New York office where he normally worked, for the ability to tell no one what had transpired, or nearly transpired, or was in that moment continuing to occur and manifest within her. As she drove, she endeavored to arrange the facts of the previous night, those she could recall, into a tolerable order. However, shuffling what she knew, from one place to the next, made her increasingly aware that the arrangement she sought was not one of chronology, but of something else, of cause and motive, fault and responsibility, and she vowed to think of it for the duration of the drive only, and planned to remove it from her mind once she reached home.

Soon after the Christmas party, Lina graduated and moved to the city, and while the company decided whether or not to hire her, she survived on inconsistent and temporary work allotted to her by an agency that kept a portion of her earnings. During this time, she questioned the path she was on, and whether it was one that would always keep her feeling so precarious and unsteady. In order to continue, she knew she had to cast the thought from her mind, and instead repeat to herself, Winners never quit, What doesn't kill you makes you stronger, and other things she had been taught and believed. When, several months later, the company did at last hire her for a permanent position, she was grateful and relieved. Her confidence in her destiny had been – as she had waited for the job – momentarily disrupted, yes, but the wait, she decided, had tested her determination and commitment appropriately, and reiterated the fact that Success comes to those who persevere.

She was apprehensive, of course, about what had occurred, or not occurred, the night of the Christmas party, her primary concern focused on keeping what had taken place, or nearly taken place, private, as she was aware it would take from her the opportunity to succeed at the company, and perhaps within the industry, if it was discovered. She had, soon after, confided in the president's assistant, telling him what she recalled, which, as she relayed it, struck her as insufficient and incapable of capturing the disquiet that accompanied it, the feeling that she was slipping away from herself. She watched the assistant at first appear remorseful, then become impressed by the knowledge that the vice president, who was widely perceived to be an impotent flunky, was capable of such actions. Finally, the assistant advised her of what she already knew, that she should stay clear of the vice president, when possible, and put the incident behind her.

On her first day of work, the president congratulated her personally, and the vice president called her from New York to offer his best wishes. He also informed her that his counsel on her hiring had, in fact, been sought, and that he could have, had he wished, opposed it with ease. There he paused to allow her to absorb the gravity of his words, to imagine in those passing seconds where she might now be, had he not been so generous. Prior to the Christmas party, like the assistant, she had thought him an inconsequential man, who, as a result of years of bullying and humiliation at the hands of the company's owners, seemed often nervous and afraid. This fear was evident in his voice over the telephone, but Lina could now also hear, embedded within it, malice and conceit. He waited for her to thank him, and she did, then hung up and did her best to remove him from her mind. There would be times, she knew, when she would have to see and tolerate him, but she took comfort in the distance between the office he worked in and hers and felt a surging need to deny him the ability to alter her course, and to think of him as merely one of the many obstacles she could and would overcome.

Lina's new boss was a woman who she quickly learned did not trust her, and perhaps did not like her, but who, because of the president's affinity for Lina, had felt pressured to hire her. Lina understood such politics were usual, and set about ingratiating herself with her boss, whom she liked well enough, when the woman was in a good mood. She enjoyed that her boss, like the president's assistant, was humorous, that she spoke loudly and directly, and laughed often. At times, her boss was rancorous and seething, and in those instances, Lina braced herself to be ridiculed or berated. While such incidents were unpleasant, she felt prepared for them. What concerned her more was that her boss did not seem to do any work, and spent her time pretending to do so, or avoiding the president, whom she also did not trust or like.

As the months wore on, Lina worried how her boss, who she was now certain did no work, could guide her on her path to learning and promotion. She began to wonder how many executives, like her boss, in the company she worked for and in others, did any actual work, and how often. But as her goal was to climb up through the ranks, and to one day become an executive, she determined it was her boss only who did so little in such a role. The president, by this time, had acquired new interns, some of who were the children of well-known and respected industry figures, and Lina understood that when the time for promotions came, they might be preferred over her. So, she did her best to work diligently when she was given work, though it was often of a personal nature and was mostly comprised of her boss's private tasks and errands. Still, it was important to Lina to keep her boss happy and focused, so that on occasion, she might be inspired to work. When that failed, she resorted to helping her boss keep up the appearance of working. She understood that the value of her own job depended on such a pretense, and that her fate was intertwined with that of her boss.

When that summer the Israel-Lebanon War, also known as the Hezbollah War, also known as the Second Lebanon War, began, Lina worried about the people who would be hurt or killed, and about her brother who had, as part of his graduate course placement, and on account of his fluency in Arabic, gone to Beirut to work. Lina's politics during college had become muted, or rather, redirected toward grievances she found abstract and aloof and without connection to her life. She was, of course, aware that her being Arab was problematic in certain spaces, and that in such instances it was enough to refrain from announcing or declaring it outright. This she had learned in friends' living rooms, and in shops and offices in which she had worked, and classrooms in which she had sat from kindergarten through college.

She did not consider herself dishonest for keeping, in her current job, her background to herself, since she was, as a rule, private, and to that effect she had absorbed the requirement to pass as one comparable to not speaking of money or lack of it, or one's political leanings, or the countless other facts about themselves she knew people juggled, and hid or presented, as needed. She had watched her own parents, on several occasions and in public spaces, silence their Arabic in the presence of bewildered or suspicious looks, and understood the necessity of such actions. Earlier internships, in addition, had indicated to her clearly and unmistakably that her passing was indeed essential to her success, and that without it, her climb, while not impossible, would become steep and perhaps without end. In particular, a French producer she had interned for, who had, as he said, a certain regard for the Lebanese, who – as he also made sure to say – were different from other Arabs, advised her that others she might work for in the future might not be as worldly as he who understood that not all Arabs despised democracy and freedom and were prone to violence and a hatred of Jews. Her decision to pass, then, was not consciously taken, but was instead natural and necessary for her desired career, as was the ability to work long hours, suffer lecherous men, and bear occasional derision.

When, after one thousand Lebanese civilians had been killed, and one million displaced, and as her brother went on land from Lebanon to Syria to Jordan in order to return home, she heard the president's assistant call Arabs animals and watched some of her co-workers high-five at the news that much of Lebanon had been destroyed and the Arabs broken, Lina felt herself an imposter. The binding that held her together loosened, and she saw herself as they might see her if they were to know her as one of the many Arabs whose deaths brought them such joy that day. She felt again as she had several times before, that what was possible and what was not was laid bare before her, but this time, however, she was alert at both the value of possibility and its cost. It was an amount, she knew, she was willing to pay, and persuaded herself to believe it was even more worthwhile, more commendable to ascend the ranks of a world that could so easily shun her.

That summer also saw the president of the company take increased notice of Lina. It began with an encounter in the mail-room, where he reminded her of their conversation the night of the Christmas party and what a rare and enjoyable exchange it had been. The value of the encounter, he suggested, was his ability to speak genuinely and openly with someone who seemed neither fazed nor altered by his status and position. Lina's esteem of the president had remained unchanged in the months since the Christmas party, despite her boss's dislike of the president, and the president's occasional reminders to Lina that her loyalties lay with him and the company and not with her boss, whom everyone knew he had been forced to hire. So, in the mailroom, Lina again reiterated her respect for the president and confirmed what she believed he hoped to hear, that her ambitions were to remain with the company and to advance her career within it.

It was common knowledge that in order for an assistant at Lina's level to gain a junior executive position, she would first be required to serve as the president's assistant. This knowledge served the president's current assistant well, as he perceived Lina to be incapable of usurping him and hence sought a future in which their promotions would be simultaneous – he to a junior executive office, and she to the president's desk. This plan the assistant shared with Lina, and it triggered within her both trepidation and pleasure. Increasingly then, she was asked by the assistant to cover his days off and holidays, a responsibility that furthered her exposure to the president, and, the assistant hoped, fostered within the president a feeling of familiarity toward her, one that could not easily be rivaled when it was time for the assistant to be promoted and his replacement sought.

So, as the summer weeks gave way to fall, Lina began increasingly to work with the president directly, and when the whispers reached her ears that soon his assistant would at last be promoted, she was certain her due would come with his. It was shortly after the whispers commenced, then, that the president complimented Lina not on the quality or ethic of her work, or even her conviviality and amiable presence, but on her physical appeal. It was a day like all others, except she was ill, and had all but lost her ability to speak. The president found her voice, made hoarse and hushed, attractive, sexually so, and he said this without embarrassment, before proceeding to ask for his messages, as if the comment had not been made, or had been and was accepted. This movement, from one comment to another, was so refined as to be nearly imperceptible, and it was only once their exchange concluded, that Lina gathered what had occurred. She sensed, however, that to investigate it, even to herself, was a dangerous act, and refrained from doing so.

Because the incident did not immediately repeat itself, with time she thought it aberrant, perhaps even imagined. She remained confident that the president, after all, was more thoughtful and dignified than other men in the industry, who used their positions to openly procure for themselves sexual favors, or who, like the vice president, tried to forcibly take them. So, when some time later, the president sent her a script, and asked her to telephone him that weekend to discuss its strengths and weaknesses, she pushed from her mind the memory of what had occurred, and spent an evening meticulously reading the script and making notes. As she did, she was aware the president's esteem of her opinion did not merit a private phone call between them. She wondered, however, if the task was, in fact, a test to determine if she was ready to take on the role of his assistant. As she dialed the number, she noted her anxiety, and how like fireworks it sparked in innumerable directions but had one nucleus. She recognized the center of her anxiety as the comment he had made and which she had worked to forget.

When he answered, he was genial but not overly familiar, and this put her at ease. She began to read from her notes, at which point he interjected and asked a cursory question about the script, followed by another. The questions she found facile, but she answered them as required, and waited. He informed her that he was to see a film that evening, and she took this as a signal that the conversation had come to an end, and she worried that their call had, in fact, been a test, that she had failed it, and that her anxiety, now clearly unfounded, was to blame. When he then asked her to accompany him to the film, she felt in her stomach a deep drop, one that threatened to be interminable, and which she knew could be halted only by her saying, quickly, before she could lose the courage, that she found such an outing inappropriate. What happened next, she would think about many times later in her life, because she would come to realize that it contained within it the very systems that structured life, made their anatomies visible and the intentions behind them clear. At her comment the president laughed, then somberly agreed. But what he sought was platonic, he assured her, and again he reminded her of their connection at the Christmas party, and also again lamented to her his position as one that placed him in what he referred to as an ivory tower which kept people like her, who were genuine and kind, distant from him. As he spoke Lina grew embarrassed at her outburst and said so, and he assured her it was expected and even commendable.

As she drove to meet him, Lina knew what was about to transpire had to be handled with great care. She was glad then, when shortly after she arrived and parked at the white high-rise in which he lived, he promptly came out, as agreed, and led her to his car. The conversation, she found, was surprisingly easy and pleasant, and it renewed in her the belief that she was, to some extent, in control of how the evening might proceed. She began to doubt not her worries, but their depth, as she could now see how her time with the president might be enjoyable, and perhaps acceptable. When she remarked that they had been driving for some time, he informed her that they were, of course, not to be seen together, as the difference in their levels at the company would deem such a sighting unseemly. On account of this, he grew apprehensive as they entered the theater, and although they were in a neighborhood far from the center of the city, his eyes continued to scan for people he might know. Only once they sat, and the lights dimmed, did he relax and appear to enjoy himself, and Lina did her best to pay attention to the film and its many details, in case the conversation to follow demanded such knowledge. When the film ended, and he asked her to dinner, she said no, and when he took her back to his apartment build- ing and invited her up, she declined and retrieved her car instead. Both times, if he was disappointed, he did not convey his feel- ings, and she again re-evaluated her assumptions and his intent.

When the following day, the president commented on her appearance and she pretended not to hear, it did not deter him. For many days after, he delivered discreetly, either on the telephone or out of the earshot of others, comments which were dispersed among the other things he said to her and were intended to disappear unless she chose to recognize and respond to them. It was then the president's assistant informed her that the president would that week commence his search for a new assistant. Lina could now make out clearly the hurdle before her, a boulder that would not remove itself from her way, and that she could not circumvent, and which she would have to confront or allow to force her to turn around altogether.

When the president sent to Lina another script and asked her to read it and speak to him once she had, and when the assistant confirmed that this was indeed the test she had awaited, she knew she would neither read the script nor meet with the president. Instead she worked to expand the distance between them, by refusing to cover for the assistant when she was able, and by taking different routes to and from the various parts of the office. When she witnessed candidates being led to meet with the president, and the assistant voiced to her his disappointment at her failure to aggressively pursue the position, Lina felt compelled to tell the assistant why this was, in the hope that he would, despite his shortcomings, and because he had at one time championed her hiring, understand the gravity of her situation. She watched the assistant, at first, appear remorseful, then become impressed by the knowledge that the president, who was known to the assistant as having once been a man desired by many women, was still capable of such actions. Finally, the assistant advised her of what she already knew, that she should seek another job, where possible, and put the incident behind her. Watching the assistant, Lina's fretfulness dissipated, and she began to see that she was not intended to succeed on terms other than the ones now spread out before her. She wondered if perhaps this path had been, despite her oblivion, clearly signposted, and whether if she had only looked down and around, instead of directly ahead, she might have seen the signs. Of this, however, she was to remain unconvinced, and she became increasingly sure the signs, while present, were never meant to be seen.

After the president hired a new assistant and promoted his old one, and after it became widely known, throughout the office, that his desires were freshly set on a young woman recently hired within the department, and that this woman returned his favor, he stopped by Lina's desk and voiced his displeasure at her lack of effort. She had not read the script he had sent, nor spoken to him about it, and he could see now, he said, that he had been erroneous in thinking she was ready for such a role. Several weeks later, when Lina entered the president's office and sat down, and told him directly and calmly of her plans to leave the company, he frowned then scowled from behind his desk, and she watched his well-groomed poise give way to a clean hate she recognized, and which she would see again many times in her life. She was making a terrible mistake, he said, and was burning a bridge in an industry in which an act such as hers was impermissible and permanent. During the tirade, Lina felt scared and uncertain, and did her best to appear calm, and said only that she was prepared to endure the consequences of her actions. This silenced him. As she rose to leave, he spoke one final time, to remind her that he was not to blame, and that he had done nothing wrong. He waited for her to repeat these words, and she did.

It was many years later, as Lina watched on television the owner of the company, accused of rape and abuse and harassment and misconduct by eighty women, turn himself in on charges pertaining to just two, that she was reminded of what she, in her youth, had experienced and felt. She did not find the news interesting or enlightening, and she was not intrigued by what might transpire between the law and the owner, who, on account of his wealth, was able to negotiate the precise terms of his arrest and bail. Even the half- and whole-hearted appeals of employees and former employees who claimed ignorance or innocence, she found tiresome, their musings inconsequential to the affected women, and the lives they led, or had hoped to lead prior to their encounters with the owner, who took from them, and of them. The women, she knew, once the excitement settled, would be the ones made to pay.

She thought of the night in the room of that expensive hotel, on that well-known boulevard, of how it had spun, of the young woman who had spun with it, and all her aspirations and desires. She became aware of the vigilance with which the young woman had put aside and away and moderated and maintained her knowledge of that night, and for that, Lina allowed herself to grieve. She yearned to reach into the memory of that room and pluck from it the young woman, to show her there were many ways to live a life, that many had not been taught to her, that she had been set down upon a path designed to ensnare her while keeping her reaching for an apex, a triumph of some kind, which would never come, and that this was by plan, not chance. But more than that, she longed to tell the young woman to carry fire, soon and often, to tell the others, and to set alight everything she saw, to waste no time burning all her bridges down.

IN THE LAND OF KAN'AN

Hayya 'ala s-salah. Hayya 'ala 'l-falah. Farid answers the call. Stands between two men who connect him to a row of two dozen others, to fourteen centuries of millions more. All facing al-Baytu l-ʿAtīq: the Primordial House, home of the Black Stone. A stone whiter than milk when it fell from Paradise only to be turned as dark as night by the sons of Adam and their sins.

He stares down past hands folded one over the other resting on his rounded belly. Eyes trace blue lines that intertwine to form the octagons and hexagons and other -agons woven through the crimson wool beneath his bare feet.

Allahu-akbar. Forward he leans. Palms on knees, back forming a ninety-degree angle with bent legs, stiff joints. The recitations turn and tumble in his mind like old acquaintances. Glory to my Lord, the Most Magnificent. Repeat and repeat.

Allahu-akbar. Up for a moment and then back down. All the way down this time. The carpet is rough against his forehead, its scent heavy and stale. He fills his lungs. Glory to my Lord, the Most High, the Most Praiseworthy. Inhales again and drinks the sweet mustiness like a newborn takes its mother's milk, all-filling, all-fulfilling. When he exhales, he can feel the breath leave his lungs, exit his mouth, but it does not blend into the air around him. Just lifts and hovers above his head, waiting to be reclaimed.

Allahu-akbar. And up and down again and two more times until he is sitting, staring at the feet of the man in front of him. The soles of the feet yellowed. The skin dry, cracked.

**

That night, you lie on your bed and stare at the ceiling. Listen to Amina's heavy breathing. You kick off the quilt, leave only the sheet. Pull both up. Kick both off. Amina mumbles and turns toward you, her eyelids closed. On her face a clear gel mask has cooled and dried. You reach out and let your fingers graze its hard, smooth surface.

She opens an eye. 'What are you doing?'

'I can't sleep.'

'Say Bismallah. Bismallah.' She turns over and pulls the quilt up to her chin. You wait for the first soft snore before you grab the khakis and navy sweater off the armchair and head downstairs. The moonlight cuts into the living room in streaks and you dress in a strip of darkness.

It's almost midnight and the street is silent. House and lawn connect to house and lawn. Glowing jack-o'-lanterns stare from their porches and stoops. Witches laugh and goblins glare as you get in your car.

Your hands steer you north on San Vicente, turn you right onto Santa Monica. Neon lights in purple, red and green. Fiesta Cantina, Rage, The Abbey. Lines wrap around street corners. Small groups walk from bar to club. Thin boys in bright tight t-shirts and stonewashed jeans tucked into leather high-tops. Men with silver hair don blazers over white V-necks that plunge deep toward sculpted chests. Broad shoulders in sequin dresses and bright blond wigs; strappy sandals lift frames of statuesque proportions.

The car vibrates to the rumble of heavy bass. You roll down the window and the beat booms into the car, pulses inside you. *Thump thump thump.* You stop at a red light. As people cross, their conversations fill your ears. You pretend they're speaking to you. *Let's go to Fubar. No, long lines. Let's go to Akbar. No, too far. Besides, everyone there has a beard. I don't want my dick scratched up by some lumberjack.* Laughter.

A young woman walks in impossibly high heels. She's flanked by two tall men whose arms link hers, helping her balance on spikes of leather and plastic. One of the men is thirty, thirty-five. He has a trimmed mustache, wide shoulders and a narrow waist. The muscles of his thighs strain against tight blue jeans. You trace the inseams up to their meeting place, haughty and defiant. Drag your eyes back up and they meet the girl's. She looks right at you and smirks. You let your eyes glide to the stoplight and stare at the red sphere.

You roll up the window as you head south on Fairfax and west on Olympic. Turn onto one street and then the next. You pull into the driveway, turn off the ignition and rest your head back as the engine cools. *Bismallah, la ilaha ill allah.* Your legs ache and your eyelids grow heavy as you pull yourself out of the car.

When you open the front door Amina's dark shape on the sofa jolts you awake. You say, 'I couldn't sleep. Went for a walk.' She stares at the keys in your hand. 'I mean, I went for a drive.' *Astaghfar allah.*

**

The first time you took him in your mouth, you were certain you would be struck dead. That baked clay would rain down from the sky and smash your skull into dust. *Indeed in that are signs for those who discern.* But in and out he went, veins throbbing with vigor, until liquid tasting of salt and metal spread its warmth and coated your teeth. So thick you had to wipe your tongue on your sleeve.

He was older. You were seventeen. They called him *Mukhannath, Manyak, Lut, Shaz.* The scar on his face ran from eyebrow to ear. His white jeans too big, held up by a belt studded with silver. Scuffed black loafers. Shoulder-length unwashed hair. A common sight on the streets of Cairo. All-around peddler. Nighttime hustler. That day, he was unloading bootleg videos. *Saturday Night Fever, Rocky, Jaws, Star Wars*. You held out money for *Taxi Driver* as he stared you down.

'That is one sick fuck.' You watched his mouth move and wondered what the stubble on his chin felt like. Became aware of a seed lying dormant in your lungs, placed there by the same hand that sent storms of sulfur to destroy the twin cities. *Astaghfar allah*.

'What?'

'The film. It's about one sick fuck.' You pretended to contemplate the tape in your hand even though its sleeve was blank, unlabeled. 'I have more,' he said. 'Come with me.' You hesitated long enough for him to hear the air catch in your throat. 'It's late now. It's fine. Come with me.'

You followed him through one cobblestone hara after the next, each narrower than the last. Past nightwomen in black lace and old men sharing bottles of watered-down zibib, milky white and smelling of fermented anise. The occasional needle passed from hand to hand to arm. *Ahlan, ya manyouk*, they greeted him. Ignored you. He fished a dinar from his pocket and handed it to a man leaning against a garbage bin in silence. Stopped to bellow a verse of Umm Kulthum with a girl who had narrow ribs and a mountainous voice.

Finally you were alone. Behind a shuttered butcher shop your mother used to send you to for liver. You leaned against the cold steel, felt the seed lodge itself into a crevice in your lungs and grow into a bulb waiting to be fed. He leaned toward you and his breath, warm and peppery, caused the bulb, now the size of your fist, to sprout shoots into the hollow of your throat. Grow stalks that reached and climbed toward your mouth and threatened to choke you in their search for air.

He stepped back and lit a cigarette. Held it out to you. 'No one comes here, relax.' The smoke you inhaled forced the stalks to shrivel and recede. He smiled at the coughs that followed. 'The first time is the hardest. After that, it gets so you need it.'

You turned toward the alley's mouth. Tried to convince yourself you had come for a movie, began to retrace your steps. He grabbed the cigarette, took a puff and flicked it to the ground, and although he was not much larger than you were, pinned you against the cool metal of the shutters. The stalks thickened and reached higher this time, past your throat and into your mouth, sprouted leaves and buds eager to bloom. He looked down and smiled. You had betrayed yourself. He reached down and caressed you and for a moment you felt only calm because you knew you couldn't choke on the petals falling on your tongue.

**

When Lot said, 'These are my daughters – they are more pure for you,' he spoke of all the girls in the town, not just his own. This was his advice to boys like you: marriage is the solution. That and salah. Salah and du'a'. Pray and supplicate. And above all, repent. Repent, repent, repent. For the ultimate transgression is the unwillingness to feel sorrow for your sins.

**

Farid wakes up next to a suitcase lying open on the bed. It takes him a moment in the gray light to make out Amina emerging from the walk-in closet with a sweater and a pair of boots in her arms.

'What are you doing?'

She lays the sweater on the bed and begins to tuck in the sleeves. 'Packing. My flight leaves at noon. Sarah is picking me up.'

Terror tinged with excitement runs through his veins as he watches her fold the sweater once, twice. He sits up, leans against the headboard. 'Where are you going?'

'To a crafts convention. I told you.'

A drip of disappointment gives way to a stream of relief. He sinks back into the pillows. 'I forgot.'

'It's just one night. I'll be back tomorrow.' She places the sweater and boots in the case and zips it shut. He watches her adjust her hair in the mirror and wants to tell her she looks beautiful, that the wrinkles around her eyes only make her more so.

She catches his stare and walks over to him, touches her hand to his. He leans up and pulls her toward him and lightly kisses her cheek. Her closed lips ease into a smile as she moves away, straightens her back. 'Don't stay cooped up here while I'm gone. Go see a movie. Take a walk. Do something nice for yourself, Farid.' Her eyes now look like his mother's. All knowing. All merciful.

**

Cairo to Los Angeles. You were one of many in the great Arab Brain Drain. Graduate college and get a job in Emreeka and with it, a wife. Given a selection of four or five to choose from upon arrival. Your father made some calls, your mother arranged the details. 'It is a blessing to marry, Farid. The rhythms of marriage make everything else easier,' she promised.

On your wedding night, Amina changed into a slip made of satin and sat beside you on the bed. Pulled hairpins from an elaborate bun until strand by strand, loose curls fell to her shoulders as you lay shaking beneath the covers. She leaned over you and held your face between her palms and kissed your cheeks. Placed her head on your shoulder and held your hand in hers for an hour and when she finally spoke, her voice was kind. 'I'm glad it's the first time for both of us. It is your first time, Farid, isn't it?'

And so it was. It is He who creates human beings from liquid, then makes them kin by blood and marriage. She took your hand and placed it on her full breast, the nipple growing hard beneath your fingertips. You stared at it, imagined that one day your son would suck life from that nipple. She pulled your face closer, moved your hand down, over a slender waist and a soft stomach. Your fingers slid farther down still, toward the patch of hair reaching up to greet them, but lingered only briefly, circled her hips and grabbed her from behind. She let out a nervous laugh as you moved on top of her, brought your face next to hers, closed your eyes and sought the streets of Cairo.

**

Farid remains in bed until he hears Sarah's car pull out of the driveway. In his robe he walks to the kitchen and sets the kettle on the burner. Twists the knob to the left until it clicks once, twice. Blue and orange flames shoot up. He watches the narrow plumes reach for the teapot, a hint of yellow visible in their centers. They are steady in their aim, intent on making the kettle scream.

He pulls out a chair and sits, stares at Amina's business guides and manuals on how to mold clay pots and make jewelry, quilt blankets and build birdhouses. The shrill whistle of hot steam jars him to attention and he rushes to the burner to quiet the sound. Pours the boiling water into a mug with a ready teabag and carries it to the living room. He draws open the drapes, letting in the ashen morning light, and after turning on the television, switches the channel to the news and mutes the sound. He walks over to the mantel and looks at the Qur'an, thick and leather bound, but does not touch it. Sets down his mug and leaves the room.

In the bathroom now, he rolls up his sleeves and turns on the sink faucet. *Bismallah.* He washes each hand three times, starting with the right. Cups his palms and fills them, pours the water into his mouth and gargles, spits. Repeat and repeat. Cleans his nose, splashes his face, returns to his arms but washes them all the way to the elbows this time. Repeat twice. Runs his wet hands over his head, around his ears. Turns off the faucet and walks to the bathtub, adjusts the knob until the water runs warm. Dips in one foot at a time. Repeat and repeat. Lifts his right index finger. *Ash-hadu an la ilaha illa-llah.*

In the dim light he sits on the sofa and rests the closed book on his lap. His fingers trace the grooves of words etched in gold into the green leather cover. Without aim, he flips the pages, allowing the book to guide him. Inside, the letters curve into one another, long melodious vowels and short crisp consonants. The harakats marked between the lines, miniature ornaments of sound, ensure a singular pronunciation. Together, the movements on the page interlace into a filigree of words too intricate to be imitated, too elegant to have been made by man. As Farid reads, his lips linger on each sound, savoring it before it leaves his tongue. Verses more evocative than poetry, more distilled than prose. A euphony belonging to no land, floating in the ether between Paradise and earth.

**

Later that afternoon Farid drives, through the flats of Beverly Hills, up Crescent and down Rodeo. He keeps to the residential streets, avoids the persistent gridlock of the main roads. His phone rings and Mazen's name appears on the screen. He slips on an earpiece and presses a button to answer.

'Mazen.'

'Hi, Baba,' the voice booms in Farid's ear. 'How are you?'

'Good, good, habibi. How are you? Are you still studying for exams?' Farid hears muffled voices in the background. Laughter.

'Yeah, just taking a break with some friends. Getting something to eat.'

Farid realizes he's driven to the end of a cul-de-sac, steers the wheel to turn the car around. 'So you're doing well? School, everything, good?'

Mazen covers his phone, says something to the others with him. The laughter moves farther from Farid's ear. 'I'm great, Baba. I was calling to check on you. I know Mama's gone. Wanted to make sure you're okay.'

Farid steers the car closer to the curb and presses down on the brake, keeps the ignition running. 'Habibi, of course I'm okay. I'm not completely useless alone, you know.'

'Mama mentioned you've just been hanging around the house.'

'I'm on vacation and Mama is too busy to take a trip right now.'

'Yeah, I know, but maybe get out a little by yourself, you know? It'll make you feel good.' Mazen's last words come out shaky, uncertain. They make Farid cringe.

'Habibi, I'm fine. I worry about you, okay? Not the other way around.'

'But I'm good, Baba. I'm very happy.' Farid listens to his son's voice, clear and bright. Feels a quiet calm spread through his body.

'Well, then I'm happy too, habibi.'

The laughter grows loud once again, fills Farid's ear. 'Thanks, Baba. I should go now. Everyone's waiting on me.'

'Yes, yes, of course. I'll see you soon.' Farid removes the earpiece and looks down the tree-lined street. Great big oaks with thick yellow leaves. He watches a cat leisurely cross the road, its gray tail wagging.

You pull your car into a metered spot near Santa Monica and Hayworth. You've never been here during the day. Driven through but never stopped. You feel the blood rush to your head as you leave your car, as your shoes touch the sidewalk. You become certain that people are staring. It takes you three blocks to notice you have passed a post office, a bank, a grocery store. Streets not unlike your own. People walk dogs. Bicyclists pass you by. Cars honk. In the sunlight, the multicolored flags seem cheerful, appropriate even.

A row of restaurants with outside seating, mostly empty tables awaiting the lunch rush, beckons you. You choose an Italian place with checkered table covers and cloth napkins. At your request, the hostess seats you beneath one of the larger umbrellas in the corner. Only one other table is filled: two men sit on the opposite end of the patio, holding hands. You make out the slight frame in a denim jacket of one, the broad shoulders and beard of the other.

'What can I get you?'

You look up at small eyes surrounded by thick lashes, curly hair shaved into a mohawk. Your hands fumble with the menu, your tongue attempts to form words. 'Yes, I – just an iced tea, please.'

You look back at the couple. The one in the jacket reaches out his arm toward the other, caresses the shoulder, touches the neck. He catches you staring. Your eyes dart down to the menu.

The waiter sets the iced tea on the table. 'Are you sure you don't want something to eat?'

'Yes, okay. How about a hamburger?'

He perks up, smiles. 'Good choice. That's my favorite.'

The man in the jacket is now laughing at something the other has said. Slaps him playfully on the arm. The bearded one grabs the hand and pulls it to his mouth. Kisses it once, twice. This time he is the one to meet your gaze. He leans and whispers to the other, the denim jacket who now turns in your direction.

Your hand starts to shake. You shove it beneath your leg, sit on it until it goes numb. Focus your attention on the passers-by. Young men in sweat shorts and tank tops. Gelled hair and smooth skin. Your lungs tighten and you start to get up. When the waiter reappears, you pull a bill from your wallet and place it on the table. 'Sorry, I have to go,' you say, not looking at him, your eyes tracing the straight lines of the tablecloth. You feel the two men in the corner watch you as you walk.

Back in your car, you sit in complete stillness, concentrating on the aching bulge in your lungs, willing it to subside. A car honks and you pull out to make room for an impatient driver waiting to take your space.

**

You sit in the kitchen with the lights off, watching video after video. Men dressed in thawbs and keffiyehs, suits and ties, khakis and polos, standing before groups large and small, speaking in prayer rooms and halls. One man calls it a 'postmodern epidemic,' another traces it to 'Western liberalism.' Over and over you watch them, excised clips posted then played thousands and thousands of times. By whom? Replayed for signs. Of what?

Yes, I bear it, this burden, sometimes high above my head like the burlap sack of a traveler and at other times low in my lungs like a tumor, but it was born as east as I was. It was born in Hara el-Hamd in Giza. And if the angels disguised as handsome boys – those who led Him to turn the cities of the plain upside down and bury their people in stone and fire – can't convince me otherwise, you, sheikhs and scholars, crooks and liars, don't stand a chance.

Astaghfar allah. Repeat and repeat.

The sharp beep of his phone jolts Farid awake on the sofa. Like pruned branches his thin limbs jut out from his belly and hang over the cushion's edge. The moon is high now and sends a single strand of light through the slit between the drapes. His eyes come to focus on the muted television, the silent news.

He reaches into his pocket for his phone, listens to Amina's voicemail telling him she's returning on a later flight. He tilts his head back, shuts his eyes and grasps at pictures, images of too-big white jeans and the touch of cold metal. Of hands that reached down and accepted what they found. Wanted it, sought it. His own hand moves down now and unzips, unbuttons. And as his breath grows shallow, his gasps for air coming closer together, he feels the small coarse grains fill his mouth. The taste brackish, the flow relentless.

ALLIGATOR

ADELE (1990)

my mother's skirt hair on my father's arms black shoes leather
sandals slippered feet across a hardwood floor strawberries
pyramid-stacked on trays crates of oranges maybe peach cha-
ching cash register louder than my mother's voice cha-ching
I'm up off the floor snatched mid-run rest my head against her
shoulder my lips on pale yellow cloth moving across the shop
her body me with it voice low sweet sings my name *Adele Adele
my lucky Adele*

White Man Lynched
By Florida Mob

Lake City, Fla., May 17, 1929.—
A white man, N. G. Romey, grocer, was
lynched near here early today several hours after his wife had been fat-
ally wounded in a gun battle with the
chief of police.

A coroner's jury held an inquest in
a ditch two miles from here where
Romey's body was found. Its verdict
was that Romey met death at the
hands of parties unknown.

The jury also found that Chief of
Police John F. Baker had acted in
self-defense in shooting the woman
five times after she had fired three
shots at Baker, breaking his shoulder
blade.

> Romey's body, filled with bullet
> wounds and sitting upright in the
> ditch, was found this morning. Au-
> thorities brought it here. Romey had
> been jailed last night.

JOSEPH (1964)

Of course we took the children in. We had our own to look after,
but they were our kin, George my cousin. He'd left Valdosta
after running into some trouble and moved his family down
to Lake City. I was doing well there. I had a grocery, not big,
but business was steady. He thought he'd do the same, and for
a while he did. I didn't ask him to come but I was glad to have
them near. Thought it would be less lonely for me and Mariam,
the kids too. If there's blame in that for me I'll take it.

For a long time after, I saw their spirits, him and Nancy both.
They weren't angry, nothing like that. Came when I was alone
and sat with me and didn't speak a word. I saw no sense in telling anyone about it. I didn't want to worry Mariam. Knew it was
just my mind seeing things and that with time it would sort itself
out. It did then, and I'm sure it will again.

We went to Birmingham after they passed. Not because I was
worried. There was nothing to run from. What's done is done,
I told Mariam, and we've nothing to get, carrying on like we've
been wronged. We'd been in the town nearly ten years. People
knew us, shopped in our grocery, said hello on the street. We're
no different from them, I told her, and she agreed. She had
a good head, that woman. God rest her.

I moved us on account of the kids. Not because I was worried. Just felt it best they grew up somewhere they wouldn't be
reminded. It would've confused them, made it harder to fit in.
So I waited until we had Samuel back, sold the shop, and left.

Dammit. Off he goes. Those pines thick as anything. Is that him there? His tail. Well gone now. That damned wind. Quiet all morning, blowing soon as I spot him, sending my scent through the pines, oaks, every goddamn thing. Should have pulled the trigger sooner. No matter.

He was big. Nine-, ten-pointer maybe. A giant for these parts. Whitetail rack shining and me not a hundred yards away. Can't get a clearer shot at this level. A wonder he didn't pick up my scent sooner. Must be running toward the cypress swamp now, startling the others. I could've pulled the trigger. Damned hand. There go the songbirds again, laughing.

No matter. The rut's cranked up. Weather's cool. More of them on the prowl. Heading toward the swamp, no doubt. Does down there. If I had my stand I would've seen him. That damned Diane. That's fine. I'll head toward the swamp, set up a blind. Might have had it set up here before I'd seen him if the hand had calmed down. It's better now. Yes. Already stopped trembling.

FLORIDA GROCER LYNCHED

(cont.)

Romey's trouble with the authorities started yesterday when Chief of Police Baker told him that he would have to clean up some rubbish in front of his store. Romey finally agreed to take some of his produce in boxes on the sidewalk inside his store.

Shortly afterward, according to

Judge Guy Gillem, Romey telephoned Chief Baker and told him he had placed the produce back on the sidewalk and for the officer to "come back and try to make me move it again."

Baker returned to the store and another argument ensued. Mrs Romey, who joined in the altercation, is said to have procured a pistol and fired three shots at Baker, one of which broke the officer's shoulder blade.

Chief Baker then opened fire on the woman, wounding her five times. She died in a hospital about midnight. Romey was arrested and placed in jail.

Sheriff (Babe) Douglas said a mob forced the lock and bars on Romey's cell. Romey formerly lived at Valdosta, Ga. He went to Florida three years ago after having been flogged by a band of masked men near Valdosta.

June 18, 1929

Dear Governor; —

I am writing you regarding the recent events surrounding the deaths of two citizens under your jurisdiction in Lake City. As you are now well aware, the Romeys met their deaths under reprehensible circumstances last month, and we demand and trust that you will do everything within your power to ensure that justice is served.

Syrian American citizens throughout Florida and elsewhere are outraged, and rightly so, at the brutality with which these lives were unnecessarily taken. Our very trust in the law is shaken, and I have faith that it can be restored only by the dutiful investigation of the men involved in this unforgivable offence.

If an investigation reflects what many Syrian Americans believe, that the policemen involved are at fault, we trust they will be duly held to account. It is only right that we pursue the course of law in this matter, not only to bring some comfort for the relatives of the deceased, but to send a message that no one is above the law.

Most respectfully yours,

WITNESS 1 – NAME WITHHELD (1968)

I'm not saying it's right what happened to that man and his wife, but it's nothing that doesn't happen to us and will again. When that mob came in I kept my head down and told the other fella to do the same. Maybe I saw their faces and maybe I didn't and what difference would it make? Men like that all look the same to me. Eyes too narrowed to see, mouths dried up and thirsty.

I was relieved enough to hear them walk past our cell and stop in front of his. Wondered if they were gonna break the lock or if the sheriff was gonna open it for them. Whether I heard a metal blow or a key turning, I don't know, and if I did or didn't makes no difference now. The other fella in the cell with me kept looking up like he was gonna see something new. He was old enough to know better and I told him so. You want them to take us too? I asked him. You want your mama to see you bruised and swollen and dangling from some damn tree?

They went on for some time hitting that man in his cell and he must've been in an awful state by the time they left. When they'd first started laying into him he was screaming loud and by the time they left I couldn't hear him no more. They had to carry him out and I'd reckon he was all but dead when they did. But I didn't look up and I didn't see nothing.

Re: 2013 Kill Thread	#43096—11/11/13 11:06 PM
bama_Bubba 10 point Registered: 02/13/11 Posts: 261 Loc: Birmingham, AL	Buck or Doe: 6 pt buck Date: 11/11 Time: 4pm Location: Osceola WMA, FL Stand location details: sitting on the ground in hardwoods bordering a pine thicket Shot distance: 125yd Distance to recovery: 50yd Weather conditions: cool and breezy Equipment used: Mossberg patriot .243 with 95 gr. Federal Fusion, Vortex scope

St. Augustine, December 31, 1840.
Glorious—Forty Indians Captured—Ten Indians Hanged.—Capt. Thompson, of the Walter M., arrived this morning from Key Biscayane, brings a verbal report that Col. Harney, who had proceeded into the Everglades with ninety men, succeeded in discovering the town of We-ki-kak, where he captured 29 women and children, and one warrior, and killed or hanged ten warriors—(they were perhaps shot in the attack.)

> We hope, however, that they were *hanged*, after being caught alive, for belonging to the gang which committed the massacres at Carloosahatchie, and Indian Key, they deserved neither mercy, judge or jury—nothing but an executioner; and the People of Florida have long deplored the unfrequency of such salutary retributive examples. If these Indians were hanged, their people will see we are at last in earnest.

CARINE (1991)

Everyone said to bear the years. Nothing but time will make it better, they said. But time's a stretched rubber band bound to snap right back into place. Lately, she's all I see when I sleep, my mother. Filling my nights with dreams that chase me well into the day.

It didn't help me none that Samuel wouldn't talk about them when they passed. Even the mention of our parents' names made him droop and fold into himself like mimosa leaves after nightfall. I was left alone with it. Over and over I thought of what fears they might've had that day, what thoughts of us they held in their final moments.

For months after, Adele cried for her mama and baba, and I couldn't tell her nothing but that they were off and away working and soon they'd come home carrying sweets and stories. She was only four, the youngest of us all, and no one could bear to tell her. How do you make a child understand something like that? No. It was for the best. Try and help the only one of us who could forget. Not a year passed before she stopped mentioning them altogether and began calling Aunt Mariam Mama even though the rest of us never did. This made Lily mad as a wet hen. 'That ain't your mama,' she screamed until Adele cried and Aunt Mariam and Uncle Joseph had no choice but to lock Lily up in the bedroom until she settled down.

When Adele passed last year I told Samuel it was only right to let Lily know. He just shrugged when I said it but he still tracked down an address, the first I'd had for her in more than twenty years. He left it to me to write the letter and all I said was she ought to come to the funeral even after all this time. Baby Adele ain't a baby no more, I said, but an old lady like us who passed in her sleep.

Well, she didn't come. And I didn't mention the letter to Samuel and he didn't ask, but I know he was thinking what I was, that she was living in Florida again, wondering how she could bear it. Even now I wouldn't step foot in that country. Me, a seventy-five-year-old woman still dreaming of her mama, frightened of waking up with her face singed on my mind's eye, her body bleeding and her belly round and sticking up in the air.

SATURDAY, DECEMBER 7, 1907

COMMISSION IS SPLIT

Members Still Differ Over Restricting Immigration.

SOME UNDESIRABLE ALIENS

Education Best Test.

Judge Burnett said last night that the only solution of the immigration problem is the educational test requiring each immigrant to be able to read and write in his own or some other language. This, he declares, will cut off 75 per cent of the undesirable immigrants, most of whom, in his opinion, come from

Asia Minor, Southern Italy, and Sicily.

"Not 60 per cent of these people can read or write," said Judge Burnett, "and it is of the utmost importance to this country that they be shut from our shores. Especially from Sicily, our immigrant is ignorant and vicious. He is coming to the United States on every steamer, and should be stopped.

Syrians Are the Worst.

"The Syrian immigrant is even worse. I found many of them who cannot even get through under our present elastic laws, and who frankly stated they were on their way to Mexico or Canada, preferably the former, in the expectation of eventually reaching the United States through those countries.

"The immigration from Germany is undoubtedly the best we get, but, unfortunately, compared with the Southern Italians, few of them are very anxious to come to this country. They are prosperous at home. We cannot get too many immigrants of the right sort from Germany, the British Isles, Switzerland, or Northern Italy, but the most drastic laws should be framed for the benefit of the Southern Italian, Sicilian, and Syrian."

Steven Morelli

October 13, 2017 at 1:43am · Birmingham, AL, United States ·

Now you all know I love football more than most guys (and gals) but the NFL is going to lose me and many others if they let these justice warriors keep this up. Their bending over backward to keep overpaid ungrateful thugs happy even if it means disrespecting our flag and anthem and most IMPORTANTLY our military the people who risk their lives to protect THEIR freedom

 39

JOSEPH (1964)

I pray to Mariam they go away soon. It was burying her that did it. God rest her soul. Going back to that cemetery, seeing their names on that stone.

At that time, dying in this country meant being buried here. There was nothing like there is now, shipping people to Lebanon, to Syria, wherever it was they were born. If you ask me, it would've been a waste, then and now. Hanging on to land that didn't hang on to you. I try to tell them that, but they don't listen. Keep me up, asking the same questions about why we buried them where we did, why the kids don't visit. Go visit them like you do me! I say.

I wanted to lay them in Valdosta. It was there they had friends, some community. But they should be in Birmingham, with us, Mariam said. Promised she'd be the one to take the kids from time to time. I didn't see any sense in it. It'll just give them nightmares, I told her, but she said she knew best. I had my hands full just trying to feed and clothe the lot of them. It was the Depression years and there wasn't much work. When George's boy and my boys were old enough to work it helped some.

It was difficult at first with the kids, but they came around. They saw it'd be different with me and Mariam looking after them. George tried, God rest him, but his trying was always getting him in trouble, Nancy encouraging him when she should've been cautioning, and him letting her say whatever came to her mind. If they'd been different they might have had an easier time, that's all. Their kids did, most of them anyway. We didn't have a whole lot to spend but we always made sure they looked right. They listened when we spoke, steered clear of trouble-makers, volunteered at church. Wasn't long before Samuel was in the grocery business himself. Two of the girls married decent men, Carine to a man named Wilson, Adele to Morelli. They got on with their lives, made beautiful families. I like to think that George and Nancy, as stubborn as they were, would be proud. I try to tell them, but they don't listen.

SHERIFF DOUGLAS – WRITTEN TESTIMONY (1929)

The persons who came into the jail last Friday and took that man are unknown to me. It was early dawn when those men came in and I was asleep on my cot in the back as is usual. I was startled half to death when I heard them come in and I ran and did everything in my power to get them away, as God is my witness. But there was too many of them and all hell bent to take that man by force. I didnt assist them in any manner and I couldnt tell them from Adam. They broke the lock on his cell and when they left I found the steel pipe they used to do it thrown inside. Its clear what happened even if it aint clear who done it.

When a mob like that is bent on taking the law into their own hands, I do my best to step in and see to it no one gets hurt. But like I said, in this particular case I cant be of much help. Who it is that took that man was and remain unknown to me.

the sun makes my head hurt bright sun two caskets the same
lowered down down Lily's face wet hand salty when I kiss it
Samuel tells her silence he runs off away Carine runs after him
comes back sits on the grass me on her lap other hands try to
lift me take me from her Carine says no no no no Lily says it too
sits next to us clasps her arms around me Carine holds us both
hums a melody I can nearly hear now how close enough to reach
no it teases and flits like lightning bugs outlines fading nothing
but highest notes and lowest can't connect one to the next

SATURDAY, DECEMBER 4, 1909

THE SYRIAN.

The contention over the granting of
naturalization papers to the Syrian is
an interesting one. The immigration
officials take the ground that the Syrian
cannot be naturalized because he is not
a white man, but a Mongolian. A Federal
Court judge in Atlanta, however, has
decided to the contrary and says the
Syrian is privileged to citizenship in
this country. The case will be taken to
the United States Court of Appeals.
The matter is an important one for the
already large Syrian population in this
country is daily growing at a rapid
rate. It is the opinion of many that
the Syrian would make a far superior
class of citizens to that of many of the
specimens from Ellis Island who are
given naturalization papers without
question. He is, as a general thing,
orderly in conduct, respectable in
appearance, busy as a bee and worships

the apostleship of thrift. The only
objection to him is that he makes too
much money.

STEVEN 'BUBBA' MORELLI (2003)

That's fresh sap. He's passed through, sure enough. But the
bark's not too ragged. Might've not been him. Some other buck
rubbing. Smaller, four-pointer, maybe five. My stand is what
I need. Be able to see clear down to the swamp, to the pine
grove where the does must be nesting. No matter. I spied him
once. I'll do it again.

A dying skill, still-hunting. Everyone and their stands, sitting
all day in the trees, waiting. On the ground like this, that's hunting.

There he goes. That's the white of him. More than fifty yards.
Can't shoot past that far. Bet he knows it. Smug and tall. A damn
giant. Hundred and eighty, no, nearly two hundred pounds. If
I get him I'll have to haul him back. How. If one of the kids had
come with me. Damn Diane. Kids and house. My damn stand.

That's right, stay right there. You're in range. Barely.

Shit. Too soon. Shit. I had to. Too soon. The legs up. He's
down. Is he? This damn hand.

THURSDAY, MAY 5, 1836.

The Indian War. — In the long letter,
which we have copied, the reader will
find the results of the march of Gen.
Scott's army, and in all probability the
results of the whole campaign, for this
season. If Scott should be equally un-
successful in his march to Peas Creek,

> all efforts to find and overcome the en-
> emy must cease until the Fall. The cli-
> mate forbids any further operations.
> It would be fatal to one-half the troops
> engaged, particularly if they continued
> to eat raw food, and suffer almost every
> other imaginable hardship.
>
> Other letters besides those above
> referred to, express but feeble hopes
> of finding the Indians — It is believed
> that they have scattered into small
> parties, and gone into the everglades.
> The troops anticipated great hardships
> on the march to Peas Creek, as the heat
> had become oppressive.

June 8, 1929

Dear Govner,

*Im a god fearing man like I know yourself must
be. And I couldnt stand by and let my concionce
eat away at me one more day. It aint right what the
sherriffs did to Romy and his wife and it aint right
what they get up to here and what lies barely baried
in front of our eyes. Bootlegin is one thing and even
making gifts of seezures were used to and look the
other way. But Romy wasnt resisting his arrest and
I saw it with my own eyes how those sherriffs beat
him with their pistols and pulled him out to the car
and his wife laying there bleeding near dead. He left
a streak of blood so thick it took ten pales of water to
clean it off. And her in no condition to be treated like
she was. I ask you if thats not criminal I dont know
what is. My mind keeps going to those poor children.
I urge you to ask those negroes in the jail to talk*

about what they saw. They will no doubt be scared to do so but I trust its in you power and interest to keep them safe.

Sincerely,

A concerned citizen

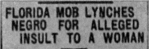

FLORIDA MOB LYNCHES NEGRO FOR ALLEGED INSULT TO A WOMAN

GAINESVILLE, Fla., Dec. 21. (AP)—Breaking the lo... jail at Waldo, 20 ... here, a party of unl... late Tuesday night... Buddington, 55, n... miles from the town to death. The neg... found by a tourist. Jury returned the v... negro came to his hands of a party... known.

FLORIDA MOB LYNCHES NEGRO CHARGED WITH ATTACKING GIRL, 12

(By Associated Press)

QUINCY, Fla., Nov. 30—Will Larkins, negro indicted here Saturday on a charge of assaulting a 12 year old white girl, was lynched Saturday night.

The negro was hanged with a strand of wire and shot to death by a mob which took him from a jail somewhere in this vicinity.

Sheriff G. S. Gregory, who was in Jacksonville, had placed the negro in an unknown jail in the afternoon. Larkins was lodged in the jail at Tallahassee Friday night for safekeeping, but it was understood he ...pirited away from there Satur... when a mob was said to have

...rida Mob Lynches Second Accused Neg...

...rry, Fla., Dec. 12 (Associa... he two negr... ection with t... Hendry, sch... last night wh... n from the o... ...pting to tra... all, and sh... ...urned at t... r a mob of m... aken him fr... ought the t...

Florida Mob Lynches Negro

QUIN...

Florida Mob Lynches Negro

MADISON, Fla., Oct. 11—(AP)—Sheriff Lonnie Davis said today that Jesse James Payne, Negro under indictment for assault with intent to rape a five-year-old white girl, was taken from an unguarded Madison county jail here last night and shot to death.

Sheriff Davis said the Negro was brought back from Raiford Tuesday to be arraigned. He pleaded innocent to the charge.

"All I know is that he was taken out of the jail sometime between dark and daylight and was found dead seven miles south of here on the highway," the sheriff said.

FLORIDA MOB LYNCHES NEGRO; SECOND CASE IN THREE DAYS

Woman Scared; She Now Tells Authorities Man Did Not Attack Her.

By the Associated Press.

LABELLE, Fla., May 12.—Henry Patterson, Negro, accused of having attacked a white woman, was shot and killed near here last night by a band of men. The body was paraded through the streets then hanged to a tree on the outskirts of town.

Patterson was arrested shortly before noon. Soon afterwards he was said to have escaped from the officers' automobile in which he was riding. Later he was captured by the mob. According to the authorities, the woman now says the Negro did not attack her, but that she was scared.

Florida Mob Lynches Insulter of White Woman

BY WIRE AND FROM...

LAKE CITY, Fla., Nov. 29.—Enraged at an insult alleged to have been made upon a young white woman of Columbia county, a party of men lynched a negro named Sam Mosely last night about ten miles south of this place. Nothing was known of the lynching until passersby on their way to Lake City noticed the body hanging to a tree by the road.

CARINE (1991)

She came to me again last night and I don't know how I mean but she was more alive than dead this time. I know in my mind it was a dream but she was talking, even laughed like she was real.

Samuel was there too and she told him to take us for ice cream. He jumped at the chance, of course. He wanted to drive the car. She called to me to take the money and when I reached out to her I noticed her smooth young hand and mine was that of an old woman. I knew then I was dreaming and it broke my heart to be older than her, my own mother.

Again she said, 'Take them for ice cream,' and Lily and Adele appeared and we ran out to the car and climbed in, scrambling over one another trying to sit next to Samuel. He got in snapping at us to sit still but he wasn't mad. You couldn't make Samuel mad no matter what, in those days. We'd barely reached the lake when the car hit us. Not hard and not head-on, just skimmed the rear right corner and scraped against the side where I sat, before taking off. We screamed then went quiet when we heard sirens because Samuel told us to calm down and we listened. He was shook, I could tell. His hands weren't steady and made the car shudder as he pulled off to the side of the road.

From where we sat we watched the patrol car follow the curve of the lake and close in on the runaway car. We wondered if they were criminals or killers or what, running away from the sheriff like that, and all we could do was hold our breaths and watch. Samuel's breaths made whistling sounds, and I wanted to hold his hand but I knew it was better to sit and wait.

After the truck decided it'd had enough it pulled over and two men, one in a straw hat, got out and began gesturing at the police. We couldn't hear what they were saying but the one with the hat whipped his arms through the air and seemed to be pointing at the sky and then the sheriffs, and I thought they would shoot him then for sure but they didn't. They just moved in on him real slow and again real slow pulled his arms behind his back and cuffed him. I remember feeling glad no one'd been hurt.

A few minutes later a sheriff appeared at our car window, telling us the truck had been stolen, apologized for it hitting us. He asked Samuel if we were all right. Did we need to be seen to?

Samuel looked around at us again and said No and waited for the sheriff to say more. Well, the sheriff walked around the car and came back to say it was in bad shape but not too bad, and that the men arrested would be liable for fixing it. 'Get the work done,' he said, 'and come see me.' Samuel thanked him and the sheriff nodded and we all waved at him and drove off.

When I woke up I spent all morning trying to remember if Samuel ever did take us to get ice cream that day or if we just turned around and went back to the store. Even now I can't decide and oh, I know it makes no difference either way. I'd just rather remember or forget, one or the other.

UNITED STATES CENSUS, 1940

```
First Name: Samuel
Middle Name: R.
Last Name: Romey
Residence: Jefferson, AL
Est. Birth Year: 1910
Birth Location: Georgia
Age at Time of Census: 30
Occupation: Truck Driver
Industry: Produce
Gender: Male
Race: White
Ethnicity: White
```

HARPER'S WEEKLY.

A JOURNAL OF CIVILIZATION

Vol. II.—No. 76.]   NEW YORK, SATURDAY, JUNE 12, 1858.   [Price Five Cents.

(contd.)

The Seminoles refused to sanction this proceeding of a few of their chiefs. The delegation themselves denied their own act, and declared that they had not signed any paper which required them to relinquish their lands or remove from Florida. They were assured that they would nevertheless be forced to carry out the treaty. Micanopy, old and inert, was little more than a tool in the hands of the bold and crafty half-breed, Oseola, who, though not a chief himself, exerted a controlling influence.

Nothing was farther from the intention of Oseola than to fulfill his agreement to emigrate. He wished to gain time, and above all things, by a display of friendship, to procure arms, powder, and lead. Thompson refused to sell these. Oseola, for a moment forgetting himself, broke out into fierce passion. "Am I a negro," he said; "a slave? I am an Indian. The white man shall not make me black. I will make the white man red with blood, and then blacken him in the sun and rain, where the wolf shall smell his bones and the vulture live upon his flesh."

Dear Governor,

I'm writing to voice my objection to what happened to that citizen in our own town this week. As I'm sure you are well aware no one is happy about the events transpired. The sheriffs were wrong to do what they did and everyone's scared to say so on account of reprisals against themselves. Some of us saw how they beat Romey with their guns and it was then his wife shot at the sheriffs and I can't myself say if this is right but I can't imagine but she thought they meant to kill him. The shot hit Baker but it wasn't him who shot her back. If you investigate you will find out it was deputy Cox who shot back several times and killed her. Everyone also knows the police let that mob take Romey the next morning. The plan to kill them was fixed between sheriff Douglas and his deputy and the police force and the whole of Lake City believes as much. They wanted to kill them because they were afraid of them.
Sincerely,
A Lake City citizen

JOSEPH (1964)

None of the ones who'd seen what happened went on record but their words got back to us just the same. I don't know if they felt bad. Surprised, I suppose. Years later the man I sold my shop to wrote to tell me he couldn't get the picture of Nancy lying on the ground of her own shop bleeding to leave his mind. I'm a Southern man and I've seen plenty of death, he wrote, but it wasn't right a white woman dying like that. I didn't tell Mariam about his letter but she found it and read it and the only thing she said was, That man wasn't even there.

How many were indeed known to us, these unknowns? How many of these men had walked into our grocery stores, sent their children to buy milk or butter or a piece of candy? How many of them stopped by for a glass of water? Said hello and goodbye and asked after our families? Some had to have been our customers, our neighbors. Some we had to have known for years.

Syrians asked the same. Didn't they know us, these men? Hadn't we gone to church with them and sat with them and made ourselves known? Surely they knew we were like them. No answer I gave was enough. Oh, they were angry. They wrote letters and hired lawyers, and I can't say that they did nothing but right by us and the children. They raised funds, collected donations and the rest. But they kept asking the same questions, and I saw they wanted to hear something I wasn't saying. That maybe it was George's fault. He and Nancy both. Surely they had brought their ends upon themselves. The law is the law and all we can do is respect it and stay out of its way. Some of them would all but say it, and nod until I did too.

THE SYRIAN WORLD

(contd.)

The details of the lynching of this Syrian are revolting. From whatever angle we view the case we can find no justification for the barbarous treatment visited by the police and the mob on this Syrian family. A full investigation of the circumstances surrounding the tragedy should be made and those responsible brought to justice. The Syrian is not a negro whom Southerners feel they are justified in lynching when he is suspected of an attack on a

> white woman. The Syrian is a civilized
> white man who has excellent traditions
> and a glorious historical background
> and should be treated as among the best
> elements of the American nation.
> — Ash-Shaab, N.Y. May 24

WITNESS 2 – NAME WITHHELD (1939)

It was just two of us in our cell when they brought him in and
walked him past us. The other man hissed at me from across the
cell to keep quiet and I did but I stole glances. They can keep
us from talking but they can't keep us from seeing is what my
grandad always said. By the time he was fifty he was well near
blind though, so take from that what you will.

This group of white men – criminals, Klansmen, good
Samaritans – roared and hollered like they were a show at the
county fair, one encouraging the other, each promising to do
worse than the man next to him. That was when I heard the
sheriff telling them to quiet down. 'Get yourselves together,' he
shouted and they did.

They seemed to have a good laugh at the man inside then but
to me it sounded like he might've gotten in a few good punches.
Then it was the sound of their boots kicking and their grunts
and spit until the sheriff again shouted at them to go. I heard
them carry him out but I kept my head down. Not because the
other man told me to. I just didn't wanna see no one with his
head kicked in, knowing his son was being kept in the back and
unable to help him none. With them gone the sheriff walked
back to his office without giving us a glance. He didn't look up
even a single time to see if we were watching.

TOURISTS HERE FIND MUSA ISLE BIG ATTRACTION

Seminole Wrestling With Alligator Always Thrills Crowd

Musa Isle Indian Village and Alligator Farm completely renewed and with many features added is again drawing thousands of visitors weekly. Musa Isle has long been the home of Florida's native Seminoles, a camp having been established there before the coming of the white man to South Florida. Today with the addition of a zoo featuring native Florida animal and bird life and an alligator farm with hundreds of the original Florida inhabitants, it is one piece that practically no winter visitor misses in his tour of the Greater Miami area.

One of the many unusual attractions at Musa Isle is the daily wrestling match between a native Seminole and a full-grown alligator. This never fails to thrill the crowds and it is a feat that not many would care to attempt.

The Indians at Musa Isle have established a complete native village where the visitor may see them living in exactly the same manner as they have for many years in the American tropics.

This, you may be assured, is a negro, not an Indian war; and if it be not speedily put down, the South will feel the effects of it on their slave population before the end of the next season.

Unless the army be placed on a better footing, it will disband; discharges are numerous, and no soldiers reenlist. The officers cannot subsist on the miserable pittance now allowed them; they should, upon principles of common justice, be placed on a footing with corresponding grades in the Navy. You, sir, will command their gratitude, and render an important service to the country, by taking the lead in this matter.

Assure the President that whatsoever promptness and energy can accomplish shall be done.

With high consideration and respect, I am, sir, your obedient servant,

TH. S. JESUP.

What happened to Pinson?	#30096—07/15/13 01:37 PM
free56hunter 8 point Registered: 11/18/09 Posts: 1785 Loc: Helena, AL	So I know someone on here will be offended and call me racist but what happened to Pinson?? I had to take my daughter to a doctor there last night and we stopped to eat afterwards at a McDonalds and as a white man, I was the MINORITY. Before we even sat down, I heard two languages other than English and saw more hoodies than I could count. Nothing wrong with different colors or other races but the people I saw definitely wouldn't have fit in the Pinson I remember as a kid.

Re: What happened to Pinson? [Re: free56hunter] #30108—07/15/13 01:46 PM	
doehunter 12 point Registered: 4/23/11 Posts: 359 Loc: ALABAMA	The apartments they built there made it real easy for thugs to move in. Not to mention the MAJOR hispanic growth over the years and even more korean and chinese. Maybe others too but those are the ones you can tell. Thing is it's not just Pinson. It's everywhere!

Re: What happened to Pinson? [Re: free56hunter] #30125—07/15/13 02:08 PM	
bh2000 14 point Registered: 10/19/10 Posts: 15823 Loc: Anytown, USA	1. How many white people are having abortions? 2. How many blacks are having abortions? 3. How many Asians are having abortions? 4. How many Arabs are having abortions? You get the idea. You have to ask yourself, since abortion/murder was legalized in the U.S. how has that affected the white population?

HALPATTER-MICCO (1836)

We faced a decision. Leave the country or fight for it. We fought. Osceola was to lead the attack against Fort King. Then he would return to help us fight soldiers approaching Wahoo Swamp from Fort Brooke. The negroes were armed and ready to fight with us. Our plan was to strike at the soldiers in the swamp. It was a safe place for us to retreat to if we lost.

When Osceola did not return, Jumper said he would lead. He would not force anyone to follow. At first light we left the swamp and approached the road. We took our positions and used pines and palmettos for cover. When the signal was given we aimed our rifles and shot dead half the white men. The half left rushed to fire cannonballs but they passed over our heads and when the smoke cleared we shot dead the men loading the cannons. They whooped and shouted and waved their swords these soldiers and officers but they had no gunpowder. At last we killed them all. The negroes stayed longer on the battlefield. They wanted to look at the dead men.

ADELE (1990)

I can hear her words so clearly my mother's words I don't know what they mean no matter how hard I listen how close they're not my words I've carried them so long before I say them to Carine what do they mean she says no no little Adele Lily shouts them back to me the words tells Carine liar you know Samuel says shhh Lily slams opens door slams again over and over she says aren't you dead yet aren't you dead yet aren't you dead yet Samuel begs stop she screams Sheriff says aren't you dead yet aren't you dead yet and I know she means my mother

TITLE: PSYCHIC P.I.
FORMAT: REALITY TELEVISION
EPISODE: AGENTS OF CHAOS
AIR DATE: FEB. 23, 2018

INT. LORRAINE AND MICHAEL'S DINING ROOM — DAY

The DETECTIVE sits across the table from MICHAEL and his wife LORRAINE.

                    DETECTIVE
          Tell me about the strange things
          you've experienced here.

                    LORRAINE
          At night, in bed, we hear sounds,
          like things are being knocked
          over, broken. But when we get up
          and check, everything's fine.

                    MICHAEL
          We've seen the outlines of peo-
          ple, dark outlines, shadow peo-
          ple. They weren't violent at first,
          but lately, there's been push-
          ing, shoving, scratches we can't
          explain.

INT. LIBRARY OFFICE — DAY

The DETECTIVE and a RESEARCHER sit at a table,
examining documents.

                    DETECTIVE
          You've looked into the history of
          my clients' house. What did you
          find out?

                    RESEARCHER
          This will be of interest to you.
          One of its longest inhabitants was
          a Lake City chief of police. Born
          in 1881, lived in the house until
          the 1940s.

                    DETECTIVE
          What can you tell us about him?

                    RESEARCHER
          He was really well liked mostly,
          that's how he became chief. But
          he was also corrupt. His entire
          department was accused of running
          gambling houses, bootlegging,
          selling women into prostitution,
          that sort of thing.

INT. LORRAINE AND MICHAEL'S HOUSE — NIGHT

The house lights are off and the MEDIUM is
illuminated by the camera light. We hear but
cannot see the CAMERAMAN.

                    MEDIUM
          I'm seeing an outline. He's speak-
          ing to me but I can't make out
          what he's saying. Wait. Gosh, he's
          saying a lot of racist things.
          Awful stuff.

                    CAMERAMAN
          Racist about who?

                    MEDIUM
          Um, about everyone. He's just
          being really racist. He's talk-
          ing about things he used to do to
          people who pissed him off, things
          he'd get other men to do to them.
          Fighting and death, really bad
          things.

INT. LORRAINE AND MICHAEL'S DINING ROOM — DAY

The DETECTIVE, the MEDIUM, MICHAEL, and LORRAINE sit at a dining table.

> DETECTIVE
> Tell us your thoughts.

> MEDIUM
> This thing, I can't say for certain what it is, but I would not call it a shadow person. I couldn't get a sense of where it came from, a point of origin or anything like that, but it was racist. Most likely what you have on your hands here is a demon.

> LORRAINE
> I felt it. I felt that whatever it was, it was evil. Its outline was dark. Dark and black.

> MEDIUM
> Yes, that was what I felt also. Very dark, very black.

> DETECTIVE
> (To Lorraine and Michael)
> Yesterday I met with a researcher who told me about a man who lived on your property over eighty years ago. He was a police chief, but he did a lot of bad things to people, some really terrible things.

>   (To Medium)
>   Could what you saw, this thing,
>   have anything to do with that man?
>
>   MEDIUM
>   Definitely, yes. I think that
>   demon, and I'm pretty certain
>   that's what it is, would have been
>   here then, and it would have influ-
>   enced that policeman to make bad
>   decisions, to hurt other people.
>   Demons are agents of chaos. They
>   make people do bad things.
>   (To Lorraine)
>   The only way to cleanse this house
>   now is to have this demon exor-
>   cised. A priest needs to come
>   here, needs to exorcise the out-
>   side of your house and then do a
>   blessing.
>
>   DETECTIVE
>   (To Medium)
>   And this will help them get rid of
>   the negativity forever?
>
>   MEDIUM
>   (To Lorraine and Michael)
>   Yes, definitely. Things will get
>   substantially better.
>
>   MICHAEL
>   This is great news.

Patient No. 34719
Location: Valdosta, Lowndes County, GA
Date of Transcript: Nov. 25, '53
Date of Revision: Oct. 12, '72

I must've been eleven, maybe twelve. My
older brother ████ took me with him and
by the time we got there they'd already
████████████████████████ branch. She was
swinging and ████████ and I'd seen a ████
████ hung like that once before but never
a woman and I looked to ██████ but he was
already pushing against the crowd trying
to get near the front. Everything smelled
like ████████ then and everything does
now. ████████ everywhere and I don't know
why they still light candles in the hall-
ways at night even though I've begged them
not to and one day they'll all go Poof!
and learn when they become flames. She was
swinging and ██████ and one of ██████'s
friends held a ██████ to her ██████ and
Poof! Ohhhhh, I kept looking, yes, why,
why, why, why, why. He ██████ her belly
with a ██████ and I only saw it fall but I
didn't hear it cry but others said it did
and they ██████ ohhhhh but I was far back
in the crowd thank God and couldn't see
thank God, god, god. Bang bang bang bang
bang so many ████ then and now still bang
too many in my head but I tell them stop
stop stop ohhhhh we'll go bang and Poof!
here won't we, doc?

Savannah, July 22, 1837

INTERESTING AND AUTHENTIC FROM FLORIDA.

We regret to learn from a correspondent, who is well informed, that there is no reliance to be placed upon the Indians; that they have no intention of emigrating. It is believed that the Micasukeys, Tailahassees, Tallopees and Indian negroes, must be exterminated before the Seminoles proper can be removed. The pacific disposition manifested by the Indians who have come to the frontier, arises it is said, from the perfect preparation which they every where observe, not only to repel their attacks, if made, but to chastise them should they manifest a hostile disposition.

Gen. Jesup, it is thought, will forbid all trading with the Indians under any circumstances whatsoever. Until an unconditional surrender takes place, & their arms are delivered up, not a single ration will, probably, be furnished, or any trading allowed. Their Chiefs, it is said, have no influence except for purposes of mischief, and it would be, it is said, the extreme of folly to trust them again.

JOSEPH (1964)

She'd heard the shot and come in holding the gun they kept in case of robberies and screamed at them to leave him be. When they didn't, she shot the chief, Baker, and he shot her back. This is what was repeated in court and the judge ruled the chief had acted in self-defense. He was right to shoot Nancy, they said, as he had feared for his life, and George killed outside the hands of the law by these persons unknown.

The private investigators hired by the Syrian newspapers found otherwise, that she was never the one to shoot first and that it wasn't Baker but the other sheriff who'd shot her down. That the whole of the incident was on account of her going down to the station some days before, asking the chief to pay to have the car fixed like they'd promised, him telling her he'd do no such thing, that he didn't owe her a damn thing and to get on her way. And that was when she called him a liar. That's what the Syrian papers said. I stopped reading those papers then. Sure enough they were working hard to prove George and Nancy innocent, but all they did was make it harder for us to get on, for people to forget. I wasn't there and I can't say but she must have thought George dead. I can't think of any other reason why she would've pulled the gun on the police. She'd come in from the shop's rear and she must've seen George on the ground with sheriffs standing over him and she must've thought him dead or on the verge of it. I've gone over it enough times in my mind to know she would've shot them then.

Either way she'd been shot, and the chief'd been shot, and that's when the kids walked in. She'd kept them hiding out back, but the shots brought Samuel out and Lily behind him to find Nancy bleeding but still alive. I wish she'd stopped screaming then. Why didn't you stop? I ask her when she comes. Why couldn't you stay quiet and help calm things down? You'd both be alive and I wouldn't be sitting in the dark talking to voices in my head.

> i was telling samuel to stand back! i was
>> screaming for samuel to stand back and they shot
>> me four more times

RE: lawyer
35 messages

Sat, Dec 15, 2002 at 3:46 AM
Steven Morelli <bama_bubba7@hotmail.com>
To: Diane Morelli <dmorelli55@yahoo.com>

Your disrespect of me knows no bounds and I know that
but the kids having to see pictures of you and whoever
your whoring yourself out to. The ink isn't even dry yet
Diane and don't forget whose paying for both lawyers
while you go out doing lord knows what. Well we know
what now don't we. What kind of mother puts up a picture
with someone like that. Your only embarrassing yourself,
he looks like a thug criminal and if you think he's going
anywhere near my kids you have another thing coming.
You should have seen Lucas face when I showed him.
Your lucky Sarah is too young to know what you are, I pray
she never does.

WITNESS 1 – NAME WITHHELD (1968)

No, let me ask you. Everyone wants to identify with the struggle
of the Black man, the Black woman, the Black child running
away from police, being killed by police. But never when they're
personally doing all right. They don't care much about us then,
how we're being slapped against this nation's asphalt, our skin
put on display to make them weep or laugh. Where were your
questions when they sent tanks into the cities, goddamn para-
troopers after us? Were you writing about the snipers killing little
girls hiding in their homes?

Look out there now, every time we walk and shout and fight
everyone else out there too, making their claim. You think anyone sends in letters when we die? You think anyone but our
own people taking issue with the police when it's us they're killing? You think anyone comes around here asking questions for

a story about some man, some woman, who died more than thirty years ago? Shit, they're not asking about the people who died today.

All right, listen. I was locked up half a dozen times before that night and I've been locked up a dozen times since and that man's screams they stayed with me until now. He might've thought himself a white man, heck, he might have actually been one for a time, but he died like us and he won't even know it. But the screams might not even be his screams anyhow. There's been too many stacked up in my mind to tell one from the other. But I know his are in there with all the rest.

Seminole Indians in Florida
by Aimee Logan, 6th grade
winner, middle school division, 1999

The Seminole Indians migrated to Florida from Alabama and Georgia in the 1700s. At that time the British called them Creeks, not Seminole, and they were a combination of many other tribes. The name Seminole came from the Spanish word cimarrón, which means wild or runaway. In the 1800s some runaway slaves from other Southern states joined the Seminole tribe and became known as Black Seminoles.

One of the most important Seminole Indians was Billy Bowlegs. His Indian name was Halpatter-Micco, which meant Alligator Chief. He was the chief of the Seminoles and he led the tribe to fight against the government in the Seminole Wars. In between the wars the Seminoles hid in the Everglades and Billy Bowlegs was called King of the Everglades. When the Seminoles lost, they had to move to Oklahoma. The chief refused to move his people at first but finally agreed. Some Seminoles wouldn't go and stayed in the Everglades instead.

The Seminole Indians play an important role in Florida's history. Many of our cities and towns still have Muskogee names, like Tallahassee and Lake Okeechobee. Many of the foods we eat now were first planted by the Seminole Indians, like corn, beans, and squash. Even some of the games we play like tug-of-war come from Native Americans.

ACT I

Dimly lit bar, several decades past its heyday. Front door to the left of stage. To the right of stage, bar counter. A barman stands behind the counter, drying glasses. On the wall behind him hangs an alligator head — mouth ajar, teeth bared. It is synthetic, made of rubber, but somewhat convincing, intimidating. Also on the wall are black-and-white photos of smiling groups of white men drinking at the bar, of white couples dancing. To the left of the counter are several stools. The only customer in the bar, Leo Cox, sits on one, drinking the end of a pint.

BARMAN:
　　　You want another?

COX:
　　　Sure.

BARMAN:
　　　(Pours another pint from the tap.)
　　　Did I tell you Derek's thinking of
　　　joining the force?

COX:

    Is he now? Well, he's a big guy, your brother. They'd be lucky to have him.

BARMAN:

    He was on the wrestling team all through school.

COX:

    Is that right? Not much fun for you, I reckon.

BARMAN:

    (Shaking head.) Sure wasn't.

COX:

    I been retired now for fifteen years and I miss it every day. Felt good to wear that uniform. Hope your brother does good by it.

BARMAN:

    He'll be putting himself to better use anyway.

COX:

    My father was a sheriff. *(Pauses.)* My family's been in Lake City for five generations, did you know that?

BARMAN:

    (Absently.) That right?

COX:

    Sure is. We helped make this place what it is. Cleared it of wild animals, savages, *(laughing)* Yankees. Even drained the goddamn glades. Cleared it and built it.

BARMAN:

>Damn shame what they're trying to
>bring down here.

COX:

>Oh, don't mind that now. People
>always go on about things changing
>but there're no changes I can see.

BARMAN:

>Derek says it's gonna get worse
>before it gets better.

COX:

>Well, he's doing his part. Ain't no
>one gonna change nothing if we don't
>let them, you tell him that.

BARMAN:

>I will.

COX:

>The history of this city is a long
>one and the only thing changed about
>the place is the name.

BARMAN:

>That right?

COX:

>Sure is. It wasn't called Lake City
>until 1859. Before that it was called
>Alligator.

BARMAN:

>*(Glances at the alligator head
>behind him.)*

COX:

> It was changed on account of the
> new mayor's wife refusing to hang
> her lace curtains in a place called
> Alligator.

BARMAN:

> *(Shaking head.)* You don't say.

COX:

> *(Laughing hard, loud.)* I always
> get a laugh outta that. We changed
> the name all right, and she hung
> her pretty lace curtains, but that
> didn't mean the gators went away,
> now did it?

BARMAN:

> *(Laughing.)* No, I suppose it didn't.

Interviewee: Betty May Jumper
Interviewer: R. Howard
Date: June 28, 1999

H: What kinds of things did he tell you about the Seminole wars?

J: He just said that they were killed by many children. They had to run and hide to keep from being killed. Then, the braves, led by Osceola fought against them and they keep chasing them down until we got to down here, at the end of the Florida state. And we went out in the glades and that is why the soldiers can't get _____- because they are scared of the snakes and the alligators and stuff. And that is why the Seminole survived. Maybe only two hundred and fifty or somewhere – survived in the Florida. That what he told me.

H: I have read some of your articles where you talk about having been a half-breed; where your Father was white and your Mother was Indian and how that put you in some danger.

J: They didn't allow the half-breeds to mix with the full-blood Seminoles in Florida, and so a lot of them have been killed – half-breeds.

H: Can you tell me about your education? Like what kind of schools you attended?

J: I wanted to go to school but they wouldn't allow me because I wasn't white and I wasn't colored. So, both groups won't take me. The colored lady who worked on a farm with my Mother told her that I could go with her daughter and she would watch me and I could go to school that way. So, my Mother said 'Alright.' But the principal was a colored man and he said, 'She is not colored. She can't go here. She is not black.'

CARINE (1991)

Once we moved to Alabama it seemed like we became different. Different people. We started going to a regular church. The service was in English only. Uncle Joseph and Aunt Mariam stopped speaking Arabic. Not completely, just to us. They spoke it to each other when they thought we weren't listening. I don't know if it makes me sad that I forgot it altogether. What difference would it have made? We still looked different enough so there was that. I'd go a year or two not thinking about it and some girl or other at school would ask me why I had hair on my arms, why I got dark in the sun. Was I sure I didn't come from colored folks? I spent years bleaching the hair on my arms, my face. Now I'm older, hardly any of it grows back anyway.

When Nick proposed of course I said yes. I wanted life to move on, to will away these thoughts now coming back each night. When my first son was born Uncle Joseph and Aunt Mariam said he looked like a real American, and he did, blond hair like his daddy, skin like cream and rosy cheeks like one of those babies in the magazine ads. For a time after, things did get better. I was busy with Nick and there were more children and I didn't have any time to sit and think, and it was just fine that way.

THE
SYRIAN WORLD

VOL. II. No. 8.   FEBRUARY, 1928

Syrian Naturalization Question in the United States

CERTAIN LEGAL ASPECTS OF OUR NATURALIZATION LAWS

A vital question which confronted the Syrians in the United States has in all likelihood been finally determined. Considerable discussion had arisen respecting the provisions of our Naturalization Act and its applicability to Syrians, more especially, Section 2169, Revised Statutes, United States Code, Title 8, Section 3599, which declared and still declares that the provisions of the Naturalization Act "shall apply to aliens being free white persons, and to aliens of African nativity, and to persons of African descent".

All others are excluded from the privilege of naturalization and thereby citizenship.

So far as Syrians are concerned, it has been judicially determined that they fall within one of the classes to whom is accorded the privilege of citizenship.

A résumé as brief as possible will be made of the several cases which discuss the question and of the decisions which settled it once and for all.

STEVEN 'BUBBA' MORELLI (2003)

Damn it, Bubba. You know better. No bad shots. Blood on the tree there. No. It's not. On the ground. Yes. And there. Not enough. Not a lung or heart. Damn it. Another drop there. Okay.

There he goes, the white of him.

No, not him.

Too white, too light.

'Hello?'

What the hell was that. There it goes again.

Scaring your damn self. Damn hand. Shakes and you feel scared is all. How long before it's tremors. Years maybe. Then what. You'll stop moving altogether. Goddamnit, don't think about that now. Focus.

That white? No.

'Hello?'

Someone else. Tracking my buck. Looks like. I'll show him. There. Two of them.

'Hey, hello!'

No. Too quick. Don't look like people at all.

Oh God.

Romance of Everglades.

The matter of the reclamation of the Florida Everglades recently has been the subject of discussion in congress. Moreover, there has been something savoring of sharp trouble for the agricultural department in the affair.

Not all the darkness and the romance of the Everglades passed with the ending of the long wars with the Seminoles, who made that region their stronghold. Semi-wild men live in the recesses of the glades today, and tragedies still frequently mark the land. Game in abundance still finds a place from the hunter in the jungles, and at least two species of birds, the Carolina paroquet and the great ivory-billed woodpecker, extinct in all other parts of the United States, have managed there to keep their race from extermination.

Defiance of Osceola.

The older tragedies of the Everglades, dark as they were, hold the most interest. It was on the edge of the jungle country that Osceola, the Seminole, when asked to sign a treaty with the whites by which the land was to be given up, drew his knife, struck its blade through the document of transfer, and said: "There is my signature."

It has been said that it takes only one drop of red blood to make an American Indian. The Everglades once furnished proof of the saying.

JOSEPH (1964)

I wish they'd let me sleep. God protect me. They come like they did that first time years ago, charcoal-black skin around the holes on her chest and him riddled to shreds like one of them paper targets on a range. Oh Mariam, take pity on me.

Don't talk about it. Don't trust no one who wants to know,
I said to the children, and Mariam said, No, Joseph, but I didn't
listen. I made her understand. She was frightened for the boy
too. You heard stories then about mobs crossing state lines to
get to the families after, to keep everyone quiet. I worried for
him, and the girls, of someone in Birmingham hearing about
it. George'd already been in trouble once, in Valdosta. Had only
a fruit stand then, nothing that could earn him enough to feed
a wife, four kids, but he worked out a way to do alright. But it
weren't long before he was brought up for gambling, running
punchboards and the like. He felt the hand of the law on him
then but he still wasn't scared. He should've been. He was an
American, he said, had been for more than ten years. He was
proud of it, said it was bound to matter if things got sticky.
I agreed. It was Klansmen who saw different.

YOU   made them forget joseph and
they   listened

I tried to protect them.
Lord knows I did
what I could.

i can't see them if they don't
speak to me

George should've learned
when those Klansmen,
when they flogged you
George for the gambling.

no noooo samuel carine
lily   adele

If you'd been quiet.
If only you'd been
  quiet when they shot you

MESSAGE TO CONGRESS – PRESIDENT ANDREW JACKSON

It gives me pleasure to announce to Congress that the benevolent policy of the Government, steadily pursued for nearly thirty years, in relation to the removal of the Indians beyond the white settlements is approaching to a happy consummation.

...

The consequences of a speedy removal will be important to the United States, to individual States, and to the Indians themselves.

...

It will separate the Indians from immediate contact with settlements of whites; free them from the power of the States; enable them to pursue happiness in their own way and under their own rude institutions; will retard the progress of decay, which is lessening their numbers, and perhaps cause them gradually, under the protection of the Government and through the influence of good counsels, to cast off their savage habits and become an interesting, civilized, and Christian community.

...

What good man would prefer a country covered with forests and ranged by a few thousand savages to our extensive Republic, studded with cities, towns, and prosperous farms embellished with all the improvements which art can devise or industry execute, occupied by more than 12,000,000 happy people, and filled with all the blessings of liberty, civilization and religion?

December 6, 1830

ABSTRACT of the population of the United States, according to the fifth census, by classes.

Total population of the United States and Territories				12,858,670

Classed as follows:

Free—White males	5,357,102			
Do females	5,172,942			
Total whites	-	-	10,530,044	
Colored males	153,443			
Do females	166,133			
Total free colored	-	319,576		
Total free population	-	-	10,849,620	
Slaves—Males	-	1,012,822		
Females	-	996,228		
Total slaves	-	-	-	2,009,050
Total United States, as above	-	-	-	12,858,670

WITNESS 2 – NAME WITHHELD (1939)

I won't pretend I thought about that dead man and his wife much over the years. I suppose if anything I thought of my own father and felt bad for that man's children, that like me they'd grow up without one.

He died when I was five, before I learned what it meant to be a man like him, black and broad and tall. He had to bend to get through the doorway of our house. His chest was wide, the length of my arm, his voice like a valley. People moved out of his way when they saw him coming. Even whites. I liked that. It made me feel safe. He was tall and strong and I felt like nothing could harm him or us because of it. All day he worked and came home smelling like oranges or grapefruit or whatever it was he'd been picking. My mother would massage his shoulders and he'd make her laugh and the both of them would fall asleep before us they were that tired.

It took ten men to carry his coffin and she walked beside it and didn't cry, even when they lowered him into ground still wet from morning rain her face stayed dry. I thought she was strong or cold but I know better now. I'd been the only one home with her when she'd been told. As soon as I heard the words I started crying. My panic got worse when I saw her face. I couldn't bear it. She looked both wretched and relieved, like she'd at last lost something she knew she'd never be allowed to keep.

I'm sorry
1 message

Tue, May 8, 2002 at 11:17 AM

Diane Morelli <dmorelli55@yahoo.com>
To: Steven Morelli <bama_bubba7@hotmail.com>

Steven– the kids told me about Aunt Carine passing and I want you to know how sorry I was to hear. I know she became more difficult in her later years but I still remember her the way she was all that time ago. She was a tough woman but kind and I know she loved you and Marcus very much. She was the closest I had to a mother-in-law and she was always good to me.

I remember when I was pregnant with Lucas she told me something that stayed with me always. She was in one of her anxious moods. Your mother had recently passed

and Carine said she was glad for her. I thought she meant she was glad to see Adele at peace after so many years of treatment. Then she told me that at the funeral she had seen her whole family there, parents, siblings, all the ones who had passed, waiting for your mother. I was surprised but not too much, you know my mother said these same kinds of things to me at that age. I asked Carine how that made her feel and she said she was glad for Adele and left it at that but I got the sense that maybe she was sad for herself to be the last one of her siblings left. She cheered up soon enough but I thought you might want to know. In my heart I think she's with them now and that she was ready.
–Diane

STEVEN 'BUBBA' MORELLI (2003)

'You sure gave me a fright. I thought I was seeing ghosts.' My laugh's strange. Did they sense it. No. Not him, her maybe. Wide faces, brown. Crouching low, that deer between them. Pretty big. A lot of blood running, even for its size. Must've pierced the heart. Didn't hear the shot. Did I. 'Want a picture?'

'No.'

Why's she looking at me like that? Big buck. Hard to heave him out of all that foliage. Even with her. 'If ya'll want some help, I'm tracking one that'll take another while yet.'

'Yeah, okay.'

More polite than her. Did she grunt? Won't look at me. Don't have to help you at all. 'I've got a good knife.' Watching me. The shot, surely was. Must have heard. Where did I? There. Don't like her eyes. Funny. Watching me, my hand. Damn shaking.

'I got one. You hold the other legs. I'll cut.'

Stubborn as her. 'I've field dressed about a dozen this big. It can get messy.'

'We got it.'

What's her problem? Ungrateful. Should walk away. Let them figure it out. A big buck. But didn't look this heavy. Two hundred pounds, maybe more. Hit right in the heart. Ask. 'What'd you get him with?' What's he nodding toward. Sidelock? No. Hammer rifle. Would've heard it. Must've. Wound smaller, cleaner than that. 'You better move quick before he bleeds out.'

'It's fine.'

That look again. Some woman. From the bottom up, deeper this time. She knows what she's doing. Strange. Steady, the blood. Not touching the meat though. She knows. Strong too. Her blade's sharp against it. In one go all of it in a thud against the ground. Strong like a man. A hammer rifle. Wrong size. Big buck. Mine must've been two hundred pounds, more. 'I've been here all morning. Funny I didn't hear or see you at all.'

'We set up last night.'

He's all right. Why's she smiling? What's to smile about?

HARPER'S WEEKLY.

JOURNAL OF CIVILIZATION

Vol. II.—No. 76.]   NEW YORK, SATURDAY, JUNE 12, 1858.   [Price Five Cents.

BILLY BOWLEGS – his Indian name is HALPATTER-MICCO – is a rather good-looking Indian of about fifty years. He has a fine forehead; a keen, black eye; Is somewhat above the medium height, and weighs about 160 pounds. His name of "Bowlegs" is a family appellation, and does not imply any parenthetical curvature of his lower limbs. When he is sober, which, I am sorry to say, is by no means his normal state, his legs are as straight as yours or mine. He has two wives, one son, five daughters, fifty slaves, and a hundred thousand dollars in hard cash. He wears his native costume; the two medals upon his breast, of which he is not a little proud, wear the likenesses of Presidents Van Buren and Fillmore.

Billy's young wife, who has no name, as far as I could learn, is a quiet, modest squaw, though her features bear a striking resemblance to those of her rakish brother, Long Jack. I was very desirous to add to my collection the portraits of Billy's "old wife" and her daughters, especially that of the elder, the "Lady Elizabeth Bowlegs," a good-looking lass of eighteen. But they "kept themselves to themselves," and very stoutly refused to have any thing to do with me or any body else.

Ben Bruno, the interpreter, adviser, confidant, and special favorite of King Billy, is a fine, intelligent-looking negro. Unlike his master, he shows a decided predilection for civilized life, and an early visit to a ready-made clothing establishment speedily transformed him into a very creditable imitation of a "white man's nigger." He has more brains than Billy and all his tribe, and exercises almost un-bounded influence over his master. The negro slaves are, in fact, the masters of their red owners, who seem fully conscious of their own mental inferiority. If a Seminole wishes to convey a high idea of his own cunning,

> he will say, "Ah, you no cheat *me.* I got
> real nigger wit." The negroes were the
> master spirits, as well as the immediate
> occasion, of the Florida war. They openly
> refused to follow their masters if they
> removed to Arkansas; and it was not
> till they capitulated that the Seminoles
> thought of emigrating.

CRIMINAL DISTRICT COURT
COLUMBIA COUNTY
STATE OF FLORIDA

– DIRECT EXAMINATION –

21 **BY MR. O'MALLEY**

22 **Q.** Please state your name for the Record.

23 **A.** Chief John F. Baker.

24 **Q.** Chief Baker, could you please tell the Court what transpired on the afternoon of May 15, 1929?

25 **A.** Lt. Cox and I went out to Romey's grocery in response to a complaint about them leaving trash out on the sidewalk. Again, I should add.

26 **Q.** So this was not the first time?

27 **A.** No, they done it on several occasions. Left produce, trash out on the sidewalk.

28 **Q.** Was it trash or produce out on the sidewalk?

29 **A.** I don't give a tinker's damn where they put their trash or their produce. But I work for the people of this town and it's my job to look into complaints. Romey had on more than one occasion left his goods and Lord knows what on the sidewalk, like it was their own personal property to do with as they please.

30 **Q.** And what transpired when you and Lt. Cox arrived at the store?

31 **A.** We asked to speak to Romey or his son, and his wife was quick to tell me neither of them were there and what's more she wasn't going to listen to a thing we had to say.

32 **Q.** And how did you and Lt. Cox react to this outburst?

33 **A.** Well, we didn't have a chance to do much before she threatened me personally, said she'd have me killed before Sunday.

34 **Q.** And what happened next?

35 **A.** I'd dealt with her before and I knew she weren't a lady at all, more of a mule, working how she did, lifting crates and breaking them down herself. It weren't natural. But I said then and I'll say again it weren't my concern. I told her to move her produce off the sidewalk and she began threatening me and gave me no choice but to take her in.

36 **Q.** Did you or Lt. Cox arrest her?

37 **A.** I did but she caused a ruckus and had people coming out their shops to see what

all her screaming was for so I let her go. I realized then her mind wasn't right to be screaming at the law like she was and I couldn't bother with her no more that day.

38 **Q.** Thank you, Chief, could you now please tell the Court what took place on the morning of May 16, 1929?

39 **A.** Well, we got a call from her husband –

40 **Q.** George Romey?

41 **A.** Yes, Romey. We got a call from him at the station and we went out there again to set things straight.

42 **Q.** What did Romey say when he called?

43 **A.** I don't know what story she might've cooked up for him about our visit. She should've been glad we'd let her go. Instead she was running her mouth and he was too stupid to shut her up. They were strange alright.

44 **Q.** Can you please tell the Court what, specifically, Romey said on the phone?

45 **A.** He was calling the law and threatening the law and that ain't gonna sit right with no one here, Jim.

46 **Q.** Were you the one to speak to him directly?

47 **A.** No, Lt. Cox was, but what difference does that make? We did our best to reason with them but it's them who decided they'd make things worse on themselves. They'd still be here breathing if they'd followed orders like everybody else.

JOSEPH (1964)

I don't know where Lily is, I tell her, but she won't listen. Lily, Lily, Lily, the two of them repeating. Please let me sleep. Lily? George on the edge of my bed weeps. I don't know where she is. Moved away. Go find her like you did me. I kept her safe, all of them. I did what I could. They kept the boy for three days. Longest three of my life. Each day going in to try and get him, and them repeating it was for his own protection he was being kept. I worried they'd hurt him, let others take him like they did you. It took letters and a lawyer to get him released and when they let him go we packed ourselves and left that cursed place for good.

Stop crying. Please God help me.

No, no, I know I didn't say your names. No talk of Zahle or Lebanon or any of it, I said to Mariam. Only Samuel seemed to remember, said one day he'd go. And I said No, you've got to get on. I said, they'd want you to get on. None of them ever laid eyes on that country. Say what you will but it's for the best.

I sent your mother money, George. I sent Nancy's family photographs of the children, and locks of their hair. I did what I knew. I couldn't go myself. No. I tried but God knows. Show your face, Joseph, I said. Go home and look George's mother, his father, Nancy's parents in the face. But I couldn't. Bought a liner ticket and sold it at a loss. Never bought another.

Forgive me.

(cont.)
Negro Prisoners Silent.

Sheriff Douglas said a mob forced the lock and bars on Romey's cell and took him away. Two Negroes who were in the jail at the time could give no information concerning the mob. Police said they were drunk and probably were unaware of the mob's visit.

FINAL DEGREE FILED IN EVERGLADE CASES LAND TO BE DRAINED

MR. BRYAN BUYS 10 MORE ACRES EVERGLADE LAND, WILL GROW GARDEN SASS HE TELLS FORMER OWNER

HALF MILLION DOLLARS IS TO BE DISBURSED BY ORDER OF COURT

NEW VAN LINE BOAT TO COMPETE WITH R. R. ON TIME SCHEDULE

Another Chapter Written in Cases of Plantation and Miami Everglade Land Companies

COSTLY HOMES BEING BUILT HIGHLEYMAN POINT ON BAY

Company Operating Service Between Miami and Jacksonville

Builds New Steamer

NEW STEAMER BE BUILT SO AS TO CROSS THE BAR

Several Residences Costing in the Neighborhood of $10,000 Each Nearing Completion

MORE MATERIAL COMES FOR FEDERAL BUILDING

Commoner Secures Title to Tract on South Fork of Miami River Near the City

INTENDED TO BUY ACRE BUT WANTS STILL MORE

STEVEN 'BUBBA' MORELLI (2003)

Big fella. Heavy even with the three of us. Looks an awful lot like. No. The damn shot though, I should have heard. Can't be.

'Thanks for helping us carry him. Not too far to the truck now.'

'Yeah, no problem.' You're welcome too. Won't say thanks once, I bet. At least he's got some sense. 'Where ya'll from anyway?'

'Here. Where're you from?'

What's with her? Damn attitude. Could drop and walk off. I should've heard the shot. 'Birmingham. My family's from near down here though, go way back.' That smirk again. Maybe something wrong with her. Damn hand, don't start now. Needs a rest. 'I usually stay on the Georgia side when I come down, camp out in Okefenokee.'

'How's it there?'

Funny way of speaking, he has. Not altogether normal either. Strange folk. 'It's not bad. Lots of gators. Gotta know what you're doing.' Is she laughing at me? Damn bitch. 'Do you have a silencer for that rifle?'

'What?'

Don't pretend you don't hear. My damn buck, and I'm helping you carry.

'Hey, the tarp!'

On the ground dirt in the.

'What's wrong with you?'

Shit. Shit. 'It's my damn hand. Fuck. Sorry.' Scrambling they are to get the dirt off, roll him back on. 'Sorry. Let me.'

'You've done enough. Please. We can handle it.'

Him next to her, like what? What, is he gonna fight me? 'You can wipe it off. It's not that bad.' Her face. His, worse. 'Just trying to help.'

'Well, no one really asked you to.'

Damn face again. Damn bitch. Bitch hand. They want me to leave. I'll just. 'I didn't even hear a shot go off.' The buck nearly back on the tarp, let him go. 'I was tracking a buck that size, got a good shot in and he woulda dropped right where I found you.' Their face like I'm the one. They're the ones, thieves. Strange fucking people, out here from God knows where. 'But I'm gonna let you have it. I worked for it, all night tracking it and waiting for it, but you can just fucking have it.'

Don't look back. Keep walking, just go. Fuck it. Thieves.

BLACK SEMINOLES (2019)

Do you know how we escaped our deaths? At times killing men who call themselves masters to save ourselves. We came from Carolina and Georgia, other places where we were tallied in ledgers, our movements counted in accounts. Again and again we went south, when the border was not ocean, when the Spanish claimed that land. For them we became Catholic and learned their words. Later we spoke Yamasee and Creek, other tongues to make ourselves useful between men fighting for soil. We took new names and became leaders. Built villages where there were swamps. Drew agreements with the tribes. At times we betrayed them, captured them for whites who told us we were better, more civilized than those running wild. At times the tribes enslaved us, hunted and returned us to whites who paid for our bodies. We married their men and women. We made children whose children survive to your present. Alongside them we fought. We founded settlements, with the Indians defeated white generals, survived wars and slave raids, and we declared our emancipation and followed John Horse who led us across this country on a stallion he called America. Is this how you imagine us?

CARINE (1991)

Oh, she wasn't afraid of nobody. She spoke her mind clear as day and you always knew where she stood. My father was the same. He was always questioning her decisions, asking if it weren't better to place the fruit farther from the fish in the shop, or why she'd again asked Samuel to move the shelves. If she felt like it, she'd respond calm enough and explain. Other times she'd announce loud and clear that she had her reasons and that was enough. Well, it went like that between them, nothing serious.

With them both in the shop most days, us kids were pretty good at looking after ourselves. We lived in the house out back so it was easy enough for them to check on us while they worked. When it was her turn to come she'd stay if we asked and she'd make us butter and sugar sandwiches. Lily loved them. I'd get her to stay even longer by telling her about something bad Lily or Samuel'd done. Or I'd get her to braid my hair because I was never any good at it. I suppose I never bothered to learn because I liked her hands on me, combing the tangles, oiling my scalp to calm the curls.

Sometimes if we were bored, we'd pop our heads through the shop's back door and if it weren't busy we'd be allowed to stay a while and maybe eat a piece of hard candy. The shop was busiest in the mornings and late afternoons. We weren't allowed there then, but Samuel convinced my parents to let him help work the shop and that meant Adele had to go too. Lily and I were too young to look after such a small child, my father said. My mother agreed and the two of them swapped her between them as they stocked shelves and served customers.

When they passed I worried so much about Adele I didn't know to think of Lily. I was the older but the difference between us was no more than two years and I must've felt like there wasn't much I could do for her. Adele was so young. Protecting her felt like something I could do. Lily scared me. Not her tantrums and shouting and fights with Uncle Joseph and Aunt Mariam. That I could handle. It was when she went quiet that scared me. Without warning her eyes would go empty and there was no way to see a thing in them then. It got so it was hard to look at her.

WOMAN LYNCHED
BY BROOKS CO. MOB

Valdosta, Ga., May 19 — Mary Turner, wife of Hayes Turner, was hanged this afternoon at Folsom's bridge over Little river, about sixteen miles north of Valdosta. Hayes Turner was hanged at the Okapilco river in Brooks county last night. His wife, it is claimed made unwise remarks today about the execution of her husband and the people in their indignant mood took exceptions to her remarks, as well as her attitude, and without waiting for nightfall took her to the river where she was hanged and her body riddled with bullets.

ADELE (1990)

dying mama you are dead I too will soon too soon they all said but no I am old young you were you'll see her there Carine says poor Carine alone mothered us all you did even Samuel older eyes waiting to die I'm afraid afraid afraid not to be dead only not to see them there maybe no there where Carine I ask where will you go so lonely to leave you says Samuel I'm here with her always Adele but Samuel his eyes I won't believe eyes with so much sadness

Steven Morelli

April 22, 2017 at 11:41pm · Birmingham, AL, United States ·

Is Hillary really still talking? Yesterday's news and today's garbage. All her talk about HER president is actually TREASON. Its like she's trying to prove the only way to silence her is to send her to prison.

 51

CHECHOTER (2019)

They say Osceola killed the General Thompson not because he had refused him weapons and gunpowder. They say it was because this general had kidnapped and enslaved me, the great Osceola's wife. They say I was a negro woman. They say I was not his wife. He shot this general with twenty-four bullets. He shot two more white men and scalped all three. These are facts not disputed. They say the scalps were divided into strips so each warrior might have a part. They say I caused the Florida War. They say I was indeed his wife.

They know he led the Seminole in battle. They know he refused to surrender. They know he refused to leave the land. He watched other chiefs surrender. He saw their people leave the places their ancestors were buried. He saw the negroes among them captured. They know his name at birth was that of a white man. They know negro blood also filled his veins.

They write he agreed to meet a general who raised a white flag in peace. They write he was betrayed. They do not write who bought me. They do not write my children's names. If I remained a slave cannot be said. I must have died but it is not written.

JOSEPH (1964)

Don't tell me anymore George
God keep you not again
                i saw it with my own eyes joseph
Don't tell me anymore
You saw no such thing
                   a woman cut up
                   naked tied to a car
No such thing
            dragged down the street where
               my fruit stand stood
Stop Oh Nancy make him
                        it was worse than that
                        worse than he says
She must've done something, she
must've hurt someone
               no
Stop I don't want
to hear it Please God let me sleep
            you too must've seen some
              yourself joseph
No I closed shop when I got wind of
them Closed and went home You
should've done the same
            i never thought then her fate
            would be mine

STEVEN 'BUBBA' MORELLI (2003)

Damn hand. What'd the doctor? First the hand, then the other
one. Whole arms later, then. Start shaking like a mad man, that's
what. Them looking at me like that. Strange faces. If it weren't
for my hand. That buck. Goddamn it. Mine to have. Damn

thieves. Where the hell they came from. I would've seen them. Last night, this morning. No, no, nothing like that. Get it out of your mind. You saw them with your own eyes. God's my witness. Shook up, that's all. Hand and Diane, the doctor and. One minute nothing and the next the two of them cutting that buck open. More than two hundred pounds. Damn thieves. Focus on the road. One hand's fine for it. I must've left something behind. No. No matter. Get some rest. For the best. I can go back. Not gonna let them scare me off. Get some rest and go back. Damn whole park's not theirs to run wild in, stealing other men's hunt. Get a bigger buck. Rest first though. Damn hand. Animals, all of them.

I Am Seminole - Everett Osceola

1,992 views

👍 36 👎 0 ↗ SHARE ⊒₊ •••

Transcript ⋮ ✕

00:00

we want to be known as how we are today

00:01

we're living we're breathing we still have

00:03

our culture we still have our language

00:04

and we want to be looked at as Americans

00:08

as well and I think for some reason the

00:11

American dream is that they forget about

00:12

the Native Americans I am Everett Osceola

00:15

and I am Seminole.

00:31

the Seminoles are called the

00:35

Unconquered people because we were the

00:36

we were the only tribe within US history

00:40

to not sign any treaties Seminole

00:44

actually was derived from a dialect of

00:48

Spanish they just said cimarrón meaning

00:50

wild one or the untamed one so it

00:54

got butchered over time and over

00:56

generations that it was called Seminole

00:57

but in a way it kind of stuck because we

01:00

weren't part of the Creeks we weren't

01:02

part of the Choctaws or the

01:03

Chickasaws we actually were a part of

01:06

some of the ancient tribes

01:07

so being untamed or wild ones you know

01:12

we just kind of inherited the

01:14

name and we have it

01:16

now and we kind of have it now proudly

06:20

we want to be remembered as how we are

06:23

now that we're living people that we're

06:26

people that are living amongst you not

06:28

something that you see in a book not

06:29

something you see on TV but you know

06:31

we're doing our thing and we're still

06:33

here and that's how we want to be

06:35

remembered is that we're still here

06:36

we're not some sort of an exhibit we're

06:39

not some sort of antique you know

06:41

extinct people you know we're still here

06:44

[Music]

Waters Rising In Everglades

Estimates Dead In Everglades Storm Close To 600 M:

New Storms Threaten The Everglades

Bu. Though Growers May Again Be Forced To Depart, They Will Go Back To Farms

The Amazing Fer' Of The Soil R:

Everglades Flood Danger Not Over, EDD Board Told

Water is now down to 17 feet, eechobes Lake level. Lamar son, Everglades Drainage Dis- chief engineer

HEAVY RAINS FLOOD FLORIDA RESORT TOWN

MIAMI, Fla., Oct. 16 in the Everglades se over Hialeah, Fla., depth of two feet, a 400 square miles of la ported.

Emergency measu save the town, wh is located, Damm iami Trail, west of ing of a ditch to into Biscayne Ba

Crops In Everglades Destroyed By Severe Rain and Hailstorm

for Federal and Red Cross Aid Sen

Storm Brings Raging Flood to Florida

Rich Crops in Everglades Ruined By High Waters After Hurricane

Photo as Page 4.

MIAMI, Oct. 12 (AP)—A small, freakish hurricane left southeast Florida under the highest floodwater in 30 years before its center swirled out into the Atlantic Sunday.

Damage from 71-mile winds was minor but hundreds of homes were isolated around Miami and Fort Lauderdale

Documents

1: *Hartford Courant* · 18 May 1929 · Page 26

2: *Los Angeles Times* · 18 May 1929 · Page 2

3: *Hartford Courant* · 09 Jan 1841 · Page 3

4: *The Washington Herald* · 07 Sep 1907 · Page 1

5: *Evening Chronicle* · 04 Dec 1909 · Page 4

6: *Fayetteville Weekly Observer* · 05 May 1836 · Page 3

7: *Harper's Weekly* · 12 Jun 1858 · Page 376

8: *The Syrian World*, Vol 3, No 12 · Jun 1929 · Page 42

9: *Miami Daily News* · 15 Jan 1929 · Page 7

10: Jesup, Thomas Sidney · 25th Congress,
2nd Session · 1837–38

11: *Gettysburg Compiler* · 08 Aug 1837 · Page 1

12: Jumper, Betty May. Interview by R. Howard. · University
of Florida, Seminole Oral Histories Collection ·
Jun 28, 1999

13: Ferris, Joseph W. · *The Syrian World*, Vol 2, No 8 ·
Feb 1928 · Page 3

14: *St. Joseph Saturday Herald* · 27 Apr 1912 · Page 3

15: Jackson, Andrew. President Andrew Jackson's Message to
Congress 'On Indian Removal' · Dec 6, 1830 · Records
of the United States Senate, 1789–1990

16: *Chicago Daily Tribune* · 18 May 1929 · Page 8

17: *Miami Daily Metropolis* · 09 Jan 1913 · Page 1

18: *The Atlanta Constitution* · 20 May 1918 · Page 1

19: "I Am Seminole—Everett Osceola." · posted by
Single Shot · 22 Aug 2017 · https://www.youtube.com/
watch?v=INWXaCjKKhc

SUMMER OF THE SHARK

I swipe my badge through the clock-in machine nearest the entrance and walk down the narrow hallway to the Pen. The rows of cubicles are still empty except for Lora's. She's already at her desk, headset on and taking a call. She watches the muted morning news on one of the TVs hanging from the ceiling and rambles in a mishmash of English and Spanish. 'Mi amor,' she says. 'Pero, you sure no quieres service in both rooms?' She's rolling her rrr's extra hard and stretching her eee's long enough to signal she's about to close the deal and it's only two minutes past six.

As usual, Max is in his office, pacing back and forth and talking at Karen. Karen's hand moves furiously across the pad in her lap, but Max's mouth is moving quicker. I know there's no way she's writing down half of what he's saying. He catches me looking and I begin to pretend I'm not, but what's the point? The man built himself a corner office made of glass and had it elevated a few feet above our cubicles so he could watch the entire salesfloor. He knows we can see him back. He wants us to.

I feel his eyes on me as I make my way down the center aisle and sit next to Lora, slip on my headset and hit 'Available' on my phone. Calls are slow coming in this early. Ten of us start first thing in the morning and groups of eight or so trickle in at the top of each hour. I like working the early shift. Lets me ease into my day and take community college classes at night.

I roll my chair back to get a better view of the TV. A red-headed woman and a doughy man wearing a checkered tie are on. The camera cuts away to Michael Jordan on the court, and as the camera zooms in, the caption reads, There's something in the air: Jordan to return as a Washington Wizard.

'Sup, dog?' Eli settles into the chair to my right.

'Hey, Eli.' I glance at my watch – 6:06. 'Were you late, man?'

'Nah, son. I almost was though. My girl was busting my balls this morning. Got all riled up 'cause I went out last night.' Eli adjusts his headset over spiked blond hair and leans back against the chair, lean pale limbs sticking out of long black shorts and a silver football jersey.

Lora twists her chair toward us, finger on her phone's mute button. 'Hey, Uh-Oh Oreo. You mind keeping your dumbass talk down?'

Eli smiles. 'Chill, baby. None of your people understand what I'm saying. Arriba, arriba, chimichanga.' Lora flips him the finger and turns back to her desk. Eli drops his voice. 'Anyway, I met this fine piece of dark chocolate last night and you know I don't like to go behind my boo, but this girl was round and sweet like a Cocoa Puff.'

'Man, you didn't.' I shake my head. Eli chuckles.

'What're you fools laughing like pendejas for?' Lora says and stands up. Her hair, dark and curly, reaches down to her waist. She walks over to the whiteboard on the back wall and marks a line beneath her name.

'You don't wanna know,' I say.

'Eli being all nasty again? At least one of you has some sense.'

Lora, like a lot of the others in the office, thinks my going to community college at night means I've figured something out – what, I don't know. At first it made her suspicious of me, made them all suspicious. They were sure I'd snitch when one of them got high during a break or hung up on a call that wasn't closing. It didn't matter how many times I told them it would be at least eight years before I graduated at the rate I was going. It took some time but she and I are cool now. She brings in apartment leases and insurance papers for me to look at before she signs them even though she can read just fine.

She grabs the remote off the partition between us and turns up the volume on the TV. The redhead and the dough man give way to images and sounds of a helicopter hovering above the ocean and fenced-off miles of sand. Lora groans. 'Not this shit again.'

It started in July when a bull shark attacked a kid playing in the water off Santa Rosa Island. The bull bit the kid's arm clean off but the kid's uncle, acting like a badass or crazed person, wrestled the fish out of the water and got the arm back. Doctors reattached it and within twenty-four hours, news crews were holding vigil outside the hospital, reporting the same three facts on loop. A week later, a surfer was attacked a few miles south of where the boy was and a New Yorker was bit in the leg while on some fancy vacation in the Bahamas. By then, the papers and broadcasters had spun themselves into a damn frenzy. You'd pick up a magazine or turn on the TV and the headline SHARK EPIDEMIC would lunge out at you. Every shark sighting, real or imagined, was reported. By mid-August, networks were showing round-the-clock footage of sharks gathering off the coast. A few days ago, a lady with bulgy eyes and wiry hair knocked on my door and asked me to sign a petition calling for legislation 'to control the problem.' I started speaking to her in Arabic until she left. I was just as confused as she was. The only words I know are either curses or orders my parents yelp at me when I'm in trouble and the way I strung them together made them lose all meaning.

My phone lets out a low tone. I glance at the caller ID and hit 'Answer' knowing it'll be fast and fruitless. You get to know these things – which area codes are buyers and which aren't.

Coughs, hoarse and dry, come through the earpiece. 'Yeah, I saw your ad in the *Pennysaver*,' a deep voice grunts. 'It says here you can put one of those satellite discs on my roof.'

I inhale loud and slow, make sure they hear it. 'That's right, ___.' I can't tell if the voice belongs to a man or a woman. 'I need to ask you a few questions first.'

'Hold on.' More coughs, slightly moist now. 'It says here I can get all the premium channels for $19.99 a month.'

'No, sir,' I guess. 'That's the basic package. Do you live in a house or an apartment?'

'An apartment but what's that have to do with it? I see my neighbor has a disc on her balcony and that heifer is watching all the soaps while I sit here wiggling my antennae.'

I want to hang up but through the glass I can't make out whether Max is wearing his earpiece. The guy has freakishly small ears and they're always tucked beneath thick black hair that looks a silvery blue under the bright lights. Makes it impossible to know if he's listening in on a call to ensure Quality Control.

'Ma'am, we require you to have a credit card to sign up for service. Do you have one of those?'

'No, but my cousin Jerry does.'

'Okay, great. You go ahead and get Jerry's card number and give me a call back and I'll be glad to send someone out to install a dish for you. Okay?'

'Well, okay. But I still wanna know about the premium channels.'

I glance at the office and spot the earpiece in Max's hand. 'Sirma'am, you get that credit card and give us a call back, okay? Have a wonderful day!' More coughs, sloppy and wet, spit at my ears as I end the call.

At ten till seven Dan comes in and sits at the desk across from me. A few others follow. I spot Tami, the only other person in the place that went to college, or tried to anyway. She'd been studying to become a medical technician but dropped out to get a second job. I take mostly biology courses. No real reason why, other than I prefer to read about things that are still alive, not dead kings and poets. We hooked up once but she had a weird thing about her being Jewish and my parents being Jordanian. Kept asking if that meant I was actually Palestinian. Wasn't Jordan filled with immigrants from Palestine? I joked about her definition of immigrant but she turned sour and I began to worry I'd messed things up. Told her I'd never even been to the damn place. I'm more American than your Polish ass, I said.

The calls start rolling in and I sell a housewife in Connecticut a three-receiver system and an old man in one of the Carolinas a basic. I glance at the board and Lora's already up to four sales. No one ever outsells her. It's how she's lasted so long – two years, going on three – longer than anyone else. Story goes Max fished her out of some strip club down in Tampa, brought her up to Pensacola and gave her a job. Felt she had a way with people even though no one can see her huge chest or the top of the *Papi Pablo* tattoo on it over the phone. Something to be said for the guy's instinct.

I'm stuck on a call with some wackjob already awake in California. He tells me his wife cut off his cable and took their pet pig. I lean back and let him babble. I could use a breather. Some sort of local variety show is on. Hostesses in polyester suits speaking in Southern drawls. The guy on the phone starts weeping and I ask him if some TV wouldn't make him feel better and he talks about the pig again, a pig named Bear. I aim the remote and turn on the closed captioning: ...*and the government is not doing anything about it. These aren't goldfish! These are deep-water flesh-hungry monsters!* The guy on the phone stops talking about the pig and starts reading me his credit card number. Makes me glad I stuck with him.

The clock ticks closer to 8:00 and another batch of people arrives. Break time. I walk outside and go around the building. Eli and a few others hang out by a picnic table next to the parking lot. A new girl with bleached hair and drawn-on brows asks me for a cigarette. As usual, Lora's in her car with the windows rolled down. She never takes her break with us. Spends it checking on her two-year-old and rambling in Spanish over the phone with whoever it is that watches the kid. Eli sits down next to me.

'Hey, son. I have some good stuff today. You want some?'

'No, man, I'm good.'

Every day Eli asks if I want to smoke weed in his truck. He's generous that way, takes whomever and smokes them out. I think it makes him less paranoid if he's not the only one taking calls stoned. I turn down the offers because I can't pull it off the way these guys do. They squirt some Visine into their eyes, eat a few mints and jump back on the phones like it's no big deal. When I'm high all I want to do is get some KFC and beat off to *America's Next Top Model*.

Eli heads to the truck with the new girl and Dan appears and sits down. His hair is buzzed close to his scalp and he wears a pair of track pants and white Nikes. Lora calls him all-American because he used to be a star baseball player in high school. Made him somewhat of a local celebrity for a time.

'I just got stuck on another call with one of your turban-wearing uncles asking for channels from the motherland,' he says.

I laugh. 'You should've put it through to me. I would've closed him.'

'No one was closing this ass wad.' He lights a cigarette and takes a drag. 'Dude, did you hear there was another attack?'

'Yeah, saw a clip about it earlier.'

'I bet you the next one will be real bad. All these hit-and-runs and bump-and-bites aren't shit.'

I take a long drag and let it out slowly. 'It's a handful of shark bites, man. I'm more scared of the wacked-out junkies on my street.'

'No, dude, it's serious. Did you see the horde of those motherfuckers off the coast? Just collecting and waiting. I'm telling you, one of those fuckers is gonna be in the right place at the right time and some dude is gonna get eaten whole.'

I get up and drop my cigarette to the ground, crush it with my heel. Dan spots a dirt mark on the toe of his shoe and leans forward and rubs it off with his fingertip. I want to tell him that the number of attacks is still lower than last year's, that my professor spent two hours last week explaining shark movements, how the swarm off the coast is part of an annual shark migration.

Joanne, a customer service rep, walks up. She's wearing pajama pants rolled up to her knees and smoking a Virginia Slim. 'Ya'll better head back in there. Max is on the prowl.'

I look at my watch – 8:12. 'Thanks, Jo.' Dan gets up and follows.

Inside, Max weaves through the Pen, making his way down each row. His face looks gray in the fluorescent light, nearly matches the turtleneck he's wearing. At each cubicle he hovers and listens to people on calls, signals them to hurry up or slow down, to upsell or come down, and when he gets really worked up, smacks the low fabric-paneled walls that separate the desks. But he never comes to a full stop. I've never even seen the guy sit.

My phone rings as soon as I put on my headset. A middle-aged woman in Arkansas needs a dish because the cable company in her town is going bankrupt. Sure sale. I'm taking down her information when Max arrives at my desk, his gray eyes wide open even though he's probably been up all night. Lora says Max likes his coca. The way he's lingering, I think he's going to listen in but he doesn't. Continues down the row instead. I look over at Eli drooping in his chair but he's already on his way to closing someone. I finish my call and look up to find Max has pulled the new girl into the glass office and is circling her as she cries. I turn to Eli. He keeps his eyes down and focuses on his call but I know he's worried.

A minute later the girl is escorted outside. Makeup runs down her face and one of her eyebrows is smeared. Max moves to the center of the Pen and spits out curses and warnings but he doesn't look at Eli. Karen stands behind him. He declares to no one in particular that he's going to get food and leaves. As soon as he's gone, everyone starts laughing and talking about the poor ex-newbie. 'Another one gone,' Eli says.

Lora shakes her head. 'Not even a warning.'

'Max is hungry today, kids,' Dan laughs.

Karen tries to rein us in but no one pays her any attention.

There's a lull in calls and I'm staring up at the TV when Dan waves his arm over the panel separating us. Eli rushes his call to a finish and the two of us stand up. 'You gotta hear this,' Dan whispers and puts his phone on speaker.

'You listening to me?' The voice is thin, raspy.

Dan forces a serious look. 'Yes, ma'am. Let me make sure I have this right, where is it you want the dish installed?'

'I told you,' the woman says. 'My husband got locked up and he can't get anything but local channels in that damn place.'

Lora stands up and Tami walks over. Dan's eyes stay focused on his phone. 'So, you want us to install a satellite dish on the prison building?'

'Yes. Can you do it by Sunday?'

Lora starts laughing and Tami smiles at me. Each of us gets calls like this every few days but only Dan invests the time you need to harvest them.

'How do you suppose we'll get around the guards and live wire fencing when we send someone to install the dish?'

'Well, how am I supposed to know? That's your job.'

'Yes, yes, it is. Well, let me give it to you straight.' Dan waits a beat. 'We do offer a special service, a hardly-used-very-top-secret machine that can shrink our installation man down to the size of a peanut. That way, he can sneak in undetected, through the fence, past the wire and into the cell. And we can shrink down a dish to go with him and he can install it *inside* your husband's TV. How does that sound?'

I fold over and try to laugh quietly while Eli snorts between chuckles. The other end of the line goes silent and Dan grins as we all lean in and wait for a dial tone.

'Ooo, you can do that?'

We erupt into such a fit that Dan has to mute his phone and take off his headset. Tami has tears in her eyes she's laughing so hard. Lora sinks back into her chair. 'Ya'll are crazy,' she says.

We start to settle down as Max walks back in. I look at the board. Only four sales under my name but it's still twenty minutes till nine. I answer a call, lean back and stare at the TV while some grandpa from Alabama, probably a non-sale, yaps in my ear. A reporter is on the beach, the Gulf stretched out behind her. The old man starts listing his order before I realize I've managed to turn him around. You go on auto-mode sometimes, say certain phrases you know will work with particular types of people.

I'm taking down the old man's address and Eli yells, 'Oh, shit.' I look at him and his face is all contorted, his nose and mouth twisting, renegotiating their positions on his face. I follow his gaze to the TV as Lora stands up.

'That looks crazy,' she says.

On the screen, dense gray smoke swells and rises from a tall building. The clock reads 8:53.

Dan turns to the TV behind him. 'Dude, what is happening?'

A caption finally shoots up onscreen, about a plane and the World Trade Center, and I hear a voice in my ear. The old man is still on the line. I want to tell him to turn on his TV but I remember he doesn't have one. This is why he called us. In the office, Max and Karen stare at a large plasma screen. Max sways from side to side.

On the TV above me the closed captions are all garbled. Eli's phone rings and he lets it go. Max sticks his head out of the office. 'Keep taking calls!' he shouts at us. Eli hits 'Answer' but leaves his eyes focused on the screen. We all do. The old man's asking me something about installation time. Lora hits 'Unavailable' on her phone, grabs the remote and turns up the volume. Dan glances up at her. 'Dude, you're gonna get us all in some shit,' he says but she ignores him.

Broadcasters report the arrival of fire crews. The redhead and dough man are back on. 'What do we know so far, Harry?' the woman asks. 'Some sort of crash, some kind of accident maybe?' 'We don't know anything really, Susy.'

Tami, Eli, and Dan go through calls, and I try to get through mine. Joanne sits on her desk and even though her headset's on, I can't tell if she's speaking. Tami finishes a call, walks over and stands behind me, her arm grazing my shoulder. We watch smoke billow from shattered windows and debris flutter to the ground like leaflets.

Joanne takes off her headset and from where she sits on her desk, she reaches for the nearest TV and turns up its volume. The jumble of different newscasters drowns out the voices on the sales floor. I try to explain to the old man what's happening, try to describe what it looks like. 'I don't care about New York City,' he says and puts me on hold to go look for his credit card.

Onscreen, the smoke is really thick and black and the redhead is giving numbers. Estimations of damages and digits of people. The time on the bottom of the screen reads 9:02 and I look down and try to focus on my half-filled order form.

The redhead breaks mid-sentence and I glance up to see a ball of fire blaze and expand close to the top of the second building. The noise from the TV now comes in shreds and fragments, interrupted gasps, abandoned sentences. A few headsets come off and several people hang up mid-calls and stand up. Eli leans back, his eyes pink and glazed. 'That is some wack shit, son.'

Max opens the office door and steps down into the Pen. 'Get back on the phones now or you're all fucking fired.' His tone is measured and booming and spreads across the sales floor. People glance down at their phones. Tami moves back toward her desk and Joanne slips into her chair. Karen picks up the remote, aims it and mutes the TV. Only Lora remains standing.

'What do you think you're doing?' Max says to her and motions as if to move toward her but doesn't, slightly tilts in her direction instead. Karen turns to the second television and begins to lift the remote again, but Lora gives her a look that stops her mid-aim before turning to Max, her dark brown eyes narrow.

'You wanna fucking fire me, go ahead, but I'm gonna stand here and find out what the hell is going on.'

The Pen falls silent except for the sound from the television. I catch Lora's eye to signal her to just let it go and sit down, to not get herself in trouble. But when she looks at me her face is like a question, and I have to look away because I know I can't do what she's asking. What would I even say? It would only get me fired with her.

Max sways in silence for an entire minute then starts to say something, loudly inhales instead, and turns around toward his office. Karen scurries to follow but he shuts the door behind him, leaving her in the Pen with us. The old man comes back on the phone and starts reading his credit card number. I don't write it down.

No one else is taking calls now and the ringing tapers off. The headline onscreen changes every few minutes until one finally sticks. The words tumble in my mind, mingle and unravel and overlap again. I know the others too have seen them. I turn to Tami and she's looking at me but glances away and back to the screen. I feel Dan's stare against my shoulders, my chest, but when I look up his eyes are still fixed on the TV. 'Fuckers,' Eli says from behind me and I don't turn to look at him. 'Dirty fuckers,' he says again. The old man's voice is still in my ear, but my neck is hot and I can't make out what he's saying.

In the office, Max sits in his chair, his back stiff and upright, and stares out into the Pen. The old man on my phone has hung up. I take off my headset and stand. On the TV they're replaying footage of the second plane. No one speaks and the phones are silent.

The shot is again replayed, once, twice. On the third time Lora lifts a hand to her mouth and her voice breaks the silence. 'Dios mío, Dios mío,' she repeats over and over, and something about how she says it, the way each word climbs over the one before, reaching for a peak, sounds like a sinister guarantee of a void on the other side.

ONCE WE WERE SYRIANS

There used to be a time when our names mattered, when being Syrian meant something else. Turn that off. They count us like grains of rice. I cannot bear it. Come closer. Listen. We used to be given things on our name alone. We would go to Abu Saadi's, my oldest brother, your grandfather, leading the way, and pick out whatever pastries we wanted. Abu Saadi's son would wrap them in red boxes and tie the boxes with white ribbons. He would write our name in a thick book his father kept next to the register. Sometimes he gave us pieces of fresh nougat, maybe with pistachios, maybe almonds. He came out from behind the counter and leaned over to hand me mine because I was the youngest. We paid with our name, you see, and my father took care of what we owed. He was an important man. His was a heavy name. People left their shops to greet him when he walked by. I tell you, they offered to drive him even when they saw him standing near his own car. He was in charge of the country's border guards. More than a thousand men worked under him. Nothing came into the country and nothing left unless he knew about it. Tall, tall he was, taller than most men, and neat. He liked everything neat. My mother washed our clothes by hand but his uniform she sent out at the end of each week to be cleaned and ironed with starch. Turn that off, I beg you. Their words cut like knives. God keep you. Listen. I read what you wrote in that essay.

Your father showed me.

Don't be upset with him. He did not want me to see. He was crying while he read it and I asked him what it was.

I don't know why he cried. Maybe he will tell you. He seemed proud, he said it was a good grade. Is that why you showed him?

Stop that. There is no reason to be mad. I thought you made many good points, God keep you. You wrote it makes you sad that people are dying, that the country might be no more. I agree with you. These things make me sad too. But you used so many words and none of them mentioned any names. How can you say what was lost without them? Our names mattered, I tell you. Without them you cannot understand the whole of it.

I don't want to upset you.

Please don't go.

God protect you, listen. Don't be mad at your father. When your grandparents moved here he was still young, younger than you are now. He was much smaller than the other boys. I knew he had a hard time. It would be even harder for a child like him now. My heart would not bear it. Back then it was only his size. He learned English in less than a year and no one noticed him doing it. Don't be mad. You can write what you like, of course. Sit with me a while longer.

God bless you. I want to tell you so you might understand, it's no small thing to lose a name. Listen, I had six brothers and sisters. Did you know that? My mother had seven brothers and sisters, my father was one of nine. We had so many cousins, so many wives of uncles and husbands of aunts. Everywhere we went were people who knew us, had grown up with our father, or gone to school with our mother, put a new roof on our house, built our furniture. Even strangers, if they asked what street I lived on, would know our neighbors. They offered us cups of tea in their shops because of it. My brothers and sisters and I spent our summers on the streets with other kids. We played football and hide-and-seek. We chased and raced each other until it got too hot to breathe. I know I am saying too much, forgive me. I know you have heard these stories, from your grandfather, from your grandmother. But maybe they were not the right ones. I will try again. We were children. We were safe.

Yes, I read the entire thing.

The end too, yes. Listen, I read what you wrote about me. This is why you ask. I am not upset. Maybe you were right to write about it, what I did. I am not proud of the way I treated that woman. But also you do not understand.

Don't be like that, God keep you. Of course I think you are smart. But this is not that kind of learning. There are some things you cannot understand from books. You were young, and I did not think you would remember her, when she came to our door with her children, when she asked for money. People we knew had sent her our way and I sent her on hers. I will not repeat the words I called her. But I tell you there was no respect for us in how she asked. I could say things were different then or I did not know better but I will not. I did forget though and you remembered. Listen, you will understand. Do you remember Damascus?

Yes, you were very young. We took you twice during Eid and both times you were still in your mother's arms. That is all right, I will remember for you. In Damascus, Eid was the best time of the year. People left their homes in the morning and filled the streets. They talked and laughed and visited people they had not seen in many months. We bought gifts and handed out sweets. We gave our good wishes to neighbors and shop owners. Every family we knew paid Muhanad the butcher to slaughter at least one sheep in its name. A third of the meat they gave to their neighbors, a third to the poor. Children dressed in new clothes and collected money from their aunts and uncles, from their grandparents. Carnivals came to town and we waited in line to go on the carousel.

It was nice, yes, and it was not nice. It was like all places. Listen. Even before and after Eid our door was open. My mother was always boiling tea and coffee, putting out sweets and fruit. People came from all over the city to see us, sometimes only to visit, other times to ask for my father's help. That was the weight of our name. Enough to forgive a debt, marry a son, maybe even save his life. Many of those who came we knew. If the visitors brought their children, we would play with them. Sometimes we were allowed to invite our own friends.

I did not have many, no. But the ones I had were close.

Yara and Lamia. And Ziad. My dearest friend.

I tell you, he was beautiful! He had a pointy chin and long eyelashes like a girl. Everyone loved him. Listen, you'll like this, the story of his birth. Everyone knew it. Ziad came out of his mother with the cord wrapped around his neck. He almost died as soon as he was born. The doctor was young and did not know what to do. He watched the poor baby turn purple. If it was not for Ziad's grandmother, he would not have lived. She took him from the doctor's hands and cut the cord so he could breathe. She told people that even after she cut it, it still moved, one last time. Can you believe it?

It is what was said, so it is what I know. But this is not the story. Listen. No one came to our house as much as Nader. He came from an old family, not as old as ours, but a good name. He was the deputy under my father, so when my father was promoted, so was Nader. This is important, always he was one position below him. It was known that Nader filled his house with things from the border, things he took for himself from searches. Televisions, radios, very expensive rugs. Of course many of the guards did the same. For fifteen years my father and Nader worked together. He was my father's closest friend. And almost every night he came to our house and drank beers and smoked argileh in our garden. I remember he had a big belly and thick fingers. He would blow rings of smoke with his nostrils to make us laugh. We liked him because he was good at telling funny stories, and before we were sent to bed we would sit with him until he told us one. I liked his voice, like music. His stories, like songs.

Who?

No, his name was Ziad. Say it like this: Zee-yad.

Very good. God protect you.

There is not more to say.

Well. Ziad's name was a heavy name, heavier than ours. His family had the biggest house on our street. My brother, your grandfather, was in the same class as Ziad's brother and sometimes he took me with him to their house. Many of the older sisters and brothers had left to be married by then. So it was a quiet house, much quieter than ours.

No, he was a year younger than me.

Rami, and he was older than Ziad. It was only Rami and Ziad left in that house. And a sister.

Her name does not matter.

She befriended me even though I was years younger.

It does not matter, I tell you.

Her hair was straight and black, her eyelashes thick like Ziad's. What else is there to say?

I don't know what she was like. She hated playing outside. She said the sun hurt her eyes, the heat made her dizzy. I was different. I loved running from one end of the street to the other and I would beg one of my brothers or sisters to use a watch to time me. I liked playing football, too, and scoring goals against the boys who would not have me on their teams.

Enough about her. She was Ziad's sister. That was all.

Not how you think, but yes, I did like him very much. I liked how easily he laughed. He was younger so we were in different classes but in the morning everyone came together for assemblies, outside on the playground, and I would see him then. I would catch him watching me and I would make my eyes bulge or wag my tongue. But I had to make sure no teacher saw. It would be two slaps on your hand with a wooden ruler if they caught you. One of them liked to yank your ear until it turned red. Ziad would try so hard to not laugh. It was funny to see, I tell you! His eyes disappeared. They became straight lines and his entire body would shake trying to keep it in.

Yes. We stood in our lines, in our uniforms, and we turned our heads toward the front. Hand on your heart you swore your loyalty and duty to the flag, to the cardboard posters with eyes that looked back at you, followed you no matter where on the playground you stood. First the father's, now the son's. Sometimes an older student sang the anthem or read a poem but no one listened to the words.

Again you ask me how we stood silent and obeyed. Why did we not shout and scream? It was not only that we were afraid. That is not the whole of it. It never once occurred to us! How do I explain to you? It would have been like shouting at the sun for its heat, at the ocean for its depth. This is what I am trying to say. Listen. Nader had only daughters. Six of them. Each year his wife tried for a boy and each year another girl with curly hair came out. Nader joked they were his punishment for the girls he had chased as a young man. He would say, 'Now I will have as many women as I tried to escape,' and then he would laugh his big belly laugh. Sometimes, one or two of his daughters came with him to visit. They were too young to play with us but still they were sent to our rooms after tea. We gave them toys to keep them busy but soon we forgot about them. We spoke openly near them. I spoke openly near them. They were only children, do you see? That was my mistake.

Whose name?

Why mention her again?

She was Ziad's sister. Her name is not important, I tell you.

Yes, I'm fine.

She did as she liked.

I am, I tell you.

Like if their maid was in the kitchen, she ordered her out. She liked to mix ingredients and put everything in the oven to see what would happen. What else? Her mother had a new sewing machine. So when she was out, Ziad's sister would go on it. She taught me how to make clothes for my dolls, for myself. I enjoyed doing that. You see, in my house I was never allowed to touch the sewing machine, or to enter the kitchen unless it was for a glass of water and even then my mother lifted the jug and filled my glass. But at Ziad's house there was no one to watch what we did, how she played. She would make a list of things for me to do. Wash her dolls and comb their hair, help her pick a dress to wear the next day. Sometimes she would mess up her bed just so I could fix it again. Even on sunny days she kept me inside. We are playing house, she would say.

What you think. She would be the dad, Ziad our son. I would pretend to cook meals, clean the house, other things I did not want to do. But enough about that.

Enough, I tell you!

I am fine. But no more about her. I want to tell you something else. Listen. Sometimes my father and Nader would be sent to the border and there they would stay for days, even weeks.

I did. I missed his height and smell but I also liked our house without him. It was louder. My sisters argued about who was wearing which dress to what friend's birthday party. My brothers put on loud battles in the living room and pretended to kill each other with plastic guns and fake grenades. Like always, my mother stayed busy cleaning everything in the house. But sometimes she came into our rooms and watched us play, or if we were outside, she changed out of her housedress and stood on our street chatting with the neighbors. Instead of full meals we ate bread and cheese, olive oil and za'atar. My mother bought whole roasted chickens and let us eat them with our fingers.

She was, very kind. God have mercy on her. I miss her still.

His way was different. He was strict.

With his hands he would measure our skirts. My brothers were never allowed to grow their hair past their ears. But he made sure we had everything we wanted. If one of my sisters pointed to a dress in a magazine, or my brothers mentioned a Lego set they had seen, all they had to do was wait. With time he came home with a package and he would smile when he handed it to us. What we got was never exactly what we had asked for, but it was close enough. We didn't ask where the packages came from or why sometimes they had on them other people's names. When he hit us it was because we had done something bad. My oldest brother got slapped across the face for cheating on an exam. My sister had her hair pulled when she cursed in the street. He grabbed her braids with his fingers, like this, and walked the whole of the living room, dragging her, repeating her curses until our ears went numb.

Don't be upset. It was what he knew.

Don't be upset, I tell you. God have mercy on him too.

No, he did not hit her. My mother he loved most of all. He brought her clothes with French labels, crocodile handbags, heavy perfumes and lace underclothes she stored in the back of her armoire. When we were home alone my sisters would take them out and try them on while I sat on the bed and watched. I was too young then to understand what clothing like that was meant to do. You might be a young woman but I bet you still don't know.

Don't laugh. It will take you many years to understand.

Her? My mother I remember like one remembers a memory. I am not sure which parts I made up. She smelled like oranges. The skin on her hands was thin, the veins in her legs bright. All day she washed and cooked and scrubbed.

Yes, all day, I tell you. I don't know how her veins did not burst, how the water did not dissolve her skin. But this is not what I want to say. Listen, so you might know. My father was gone for weeks before I noticed how our neighbors no longer looked us directly in the eyes. Still I asked my mother nothing. None of us did. Instead a quiet filled our home, so heavy I wish it not even on the dead. We ate without making a sound. We became full with silence. Each day that summer I sat by the window that looked down on our street and watched the corner where it crossed the main road. I tried to make him appear, you see? I promised myself if I held my breath for ten seconds longer or didn't blink for fifteen counts more, I would see him come around the corner in his uniform. I imagined him walking to the house and lifting his hand to wave at me. I still did not know then the mistake I had made.

How do I explain to you? In our homes things were thought instead of spoken. Our neighbors, who we laughed with, who we had over for lunch, exchanged desserts with after dinner, whose youngest children we helped feed on our laps, were separated from us by walls we could see and walls we could not. We did not know who would speak, what stories about us real or made up they would tell to gain what they could. Or worse, because they had no other choice, because maybe it meant their lives instead. Once, when I was seven, maybe eight, my friend Yara came over and I began to tell her about a trip to the coast my family had taken, a weekend in Latakia. I told her how the sun burned my shoulders, how I had to put yogurt on my skin and spend the rest of my time under a parasol. But as soon as I began to tell her where we stayed, who we visited, my mother appeared in the doorway. I saw her face and somehow I knew to stop. I turned to Yara and asked her if she preferred to paint or draw. That time, I knew to stop. Are you beginning to understand?

Good. God bless you. God protect you. Do you know I saw her again? Nine, ten years ago. But she did not remember me.

No, no. Not Yara. Ziad's sister. I saw Ziad's sister at a wedding, Muhsain and Jumana's wedding. I never told anyone. You were there but very young, too young to remember how she reached out and touched your hair. She petted you like a mouse. My hand shook when she took it. She introduced herself, as if I did not know who she was! Even my name made her remember nothing. During the dinner I sat where I could see the back of her head. Her hair was still thick and black. Mine was already gray by then. Only when the dancing ended and the music stopped and I saw her stand up I approached her again. I pretended I had only just remembered. I named our street and all our neighbors, asked about Ziad and the rest of her family. She stared at me with her blue eyes and shook her head. 'I am sorry,' she said, 'I do not remember.' I cannot imagine what my face must have looked like, I tell you, because one of Jumana's cousins came to me then and apologized. 'Oh, she had an accident after her marriage,' the cousin said. 'Her memory is not good.' I wanted to ask about the accident, where the husband was, but I stayed quiet and she walked away.

No, no. I am not upset. But she should have remembered.

I am not upset, I tell you.

Enough! I beg you. I was telling a different story. Why remember her? I am becoming an old lady telling stories this way. God give you patience. Where was I?

Yes. God keep you. Listen. When my father was released it was to a hospital and when he came home it was in the middle of the night. For many weeks we told the neighbors he was ill, that he had caught a strange flu at the border. They nodded. Not to say they believed, you see, but that they agreed it was a good story. In all that time he stayed in his room. My mother alone kept us fed and warm. To this day I cannot tell you how. She fed us in the mornings and sat with him until lunch. We stood at their closed door and held our breaths to hear what we could, but we never heard even a word. It was like they too were holding their breaths.

With time he did, if only to sit in the garden. But it felt like our name was no more. Even our closest neighbors stayed away.

Of course, we understood. My father understood best of all. He stayed home, where no one could see him, inside or in the garden. But not because he was afraid, understand. It kept those who would have spoken to him, the people who might feel they had to greet him, safe. God have mercy on him.

He grew quieter. Shorter, somehow, without his uniform. It was strange to see him in civilian clothes, but we grew used to it.

We did, yes. But only many years later. Long after he and my mother had both died and were buried side by side, God have mercy on them. It was then one of Nader's daughters came to ask our forgiveness. But there was nothing to forgive. The mistake was mine as much as it was hers. It would have been like blaming the wood that makes the hammer's handle, or the yarn fed through the spinner's wheel. Do you understand?

Good, because I need to explain, so you might know, because I like that you are not silent. You are loud.

You are, I tell you. They say the pen is one of the two tongues. In the essay you are loud.

Listen. I beg you! You wrote it makes you sad that Syria might be no more. It is sad, yes, but there is more to it. On the television, in the newspapers, they speak of countries like they are no more than lines on a paper. We had names, I tell you. And while we sat in classrooms, and exchanged notes, and asked our mothers for coins to buy treats from the peddler on our street, people in places we had never seen were busy making borders and drawing lines between our names. Listen. I sent that woman away that day, with her children behind her, because I thought I was better than her, an Iraqi, a peasant, a refugee. That is what I called her. I no longer had my name but I was Syrian and I was better. Do you understand? I did not draw the line but all my life I followed it.

Please listen. I am almost finished.

What do you want to know?

Yes, we stayed. There was nowhere else to go. My father would not have been allowed to leave.

Like I said, I never had many. But yes, most of them stopped speaking to me. I thought of them as my friends still. I understood.

Oh, yes, he did. Ziad was different. It was not that he was braver than the others, no. I did not understand then, but now I know he needed to. It was his way.

His way to apologize.

No, not just for what had happened to my father. More than that. I cannot explain. But when his parents were out he would come to our garden and sit until someone noticed him and called for me. If my father was there the two of them greeted each other quietly. With time, things got better. My father died, then my mother. God have mercy on them. People pretended to forget.

Pretending is the same as forgetting, I tell you. It made it so we could leave. Listen, those people who protested.

It is for more than your essay. Please. Those people, who protested, they went out on the streets with nothing but their clothes, they kept going even when the snipers shot at them, killed them, even. This was not to change a president or to find a democracy. Write what you like, but please know it is not the whole of it. The government took fifteen children. They placed them in cells and whipped them like cattle for writing words on stone. It was not the first time or the worst time, but it is the drop that makes the dam overflow. People spilled onto the streets and for the first time in fifty years they did not whisper. They shouted! They sang! They heard the sounds of their own voices. How were they to be made quiet again? It was impossible, I tell you. Even here, so far away, we shook from shock, not fear. It was like hearing that what we thought was the sun was only the moon, that the sky we believed to be blue was in fact red. Please understand! Who can count if what was gained is more or less than what was lost? Who would dare try? My heart grieves for them.

Yes, I am all right. God keep you. You are good to listen.

No, Ziad never left. Even when there was still a chance, even when so many did. I grieve for him too. He was my friend.

We did, yes. After I left he sent me letters. The final one came not long after the first protest. It had only one line.

'I wish it had not taken me so long to find my voice.'

Yes, but he did not mean only that. I know you do not understand. I am not sure I can make you.

I do not know how to try.

I am fine.

I do want to.

Listen. Listen so I can try. Ziad's sister liked to play house. She would be the husband. I would be the wife.

Yes, yes. I'm okay.

Her the husband. Me the wife. She made Ziad pretend to be our son.

Please, listen, while I can. She would make me the wife. Tell me to cook the pretend meals. Stuffed zucchini, green bean stew. She helped Ziad with pretend homework. She was the husband.

I am, please listen. She would close the curtains in her room. Heavy curtains, curtains that made it dark like night even in midday. Time for bed, she would say. She would put blankets on the floor of her closet for Ziad then shut the door. That was his pretend room. Then she would get into the bed and tell me to get in with her. I did not want to but I did.

Do not be upset. Listen, what can it matter now?

He did not, no. He did not open the door once. He was good, he stayed quiet.

Yes, he knew. But we never spoke of it. What would we have said?

We did not have these words.

Who would I have told? Theirs was a heavy name, much heavier than ours.

No.

No, I say.

I will try. For you only.

Zaynab. Her name was Zaynab. That is enough now. There is no more to say.

I am fine. Don't be upset. Please, I am. I will be. It feels good to speak. Listen, I am no longer sure one story is worse than the other.

I am saying her, and Nader, they are the same story in the end. You say this even in your essay.

You do, I tell you. I understand now.

You wrote about what has happened to Syrians, about the Iraqi woman and me. I see now they were also the same story. You and I, we are telling only one story.

You will understand. I know this now. God bless you. It is a good essay, God protect you, I hope you are always this loud.

Listen. Do you know my mother took her name with her to her grave? She was the last of her family to die, God have mercy on her, and there were no grandsons in that family to carry the name. One of my uncles did not have children. Another had only girls. A third died as a child. Why did I not mourn her name, my own mother, the way I still mourn ours?

Yes, yes. You are right. It is her father's name. I do not know the answer. God keep you, I think you might find another way. Already you are. But so many names are gone. Killed or moved, spread across the world. What they mean will change. I thought this was only bad and now I cannot say. I do not know what they will become, what I will become with them. You will decide. When I answered the door to that woman, I was Syrian. This is not right or wrong. But I beg you, what do they call me now?

Nadia L.

Ms. Sheehan

English 2H

The Syrian Refugee Crisis

Syria is a country that borders Lebanon, Turkey, Jordan, and Israel. Before the civil war, Syria's population was 20 million people. Now it's half of that. From 1516 to 1920 Syria was part of the Ottoman Empire. In 1920 Britain and France divided it into different countries that include Syria, Lebanon, Palestine, and part of Jordan. France controlled Syria until 1948. In 1958 Syria formed a country with Egypt, but that ended in 1961 because the Syrian people did not want to be controlled by Egypt. The Ba'ath Party and the al-Assads have controlled it since then.

The civil war began in 2011 because the Syrian people tried to overthrow the president. They wanted democracy and freedom and they were inspired by revolutions in other Arab countries. The president's family had controlled the country for almost 50 years. It can be hard to understand why the people in Syria allowed this to happen but I think they were afraid of being killed.

My father is from Syria and he moved here before I was born. He came with his family as a kid because his dad got a job in San Francisco and also because his dad's sister was already living here. When my dad watches the news about Syria he gets angry and sad. He is mad at Russia and Iran and al-Assad for killing so many people and making so many refugees. But he is mostly sad at the rest of the world for not doing anything to stop it. I feel sad for him that he might not be able to go there ever again and that Syria might not even be a country one day.

Because of the war many Syrians have escaped and gone to other countries. There are about seven million Syrian refugees in Turkey, Lebanon, and Jordan and one million in Europe. Most countries do not want refugees because they're afraid they will take their jobs and cause crime. In Psychology we learned that people are more likely to help people who are like them. For example, if they are the same race or gender or speak the same language. My mom thinks that if people thought of Syrians as more like them then they might want to help. She makes a point to tell people that I'm half Syrian or that she is married to a Syrian. I think it will take more than that. When I was little a woman came to our house with her children when my great-aunt was babysitting me. She spoke to my great-aunt in Arabic and even though I don't speak a lot of Arabic I could tell she was asking her for money. I felt bad for the kids because their clothes looked old and they were really quiet. My great-aunt did not give her money and sent her away. I think what this shows is that even speaking the same language is not enough sometimes.

A lot of research has been done on what refugees can cost a country and how much they can also benefit a country. In my opinion, this research is strange because when a person is born, we don't add up what they cost or how much money they'll make later in life. In the future I would like to do something that helps refugees from not just Syria but from all over the world. What should be important is not where people are from or how much money they have. All that should matter is that they are in danger. It is up to us who are not in danger to help.

A GIRL IN THREE ACTS

I

Girl's grandfather died inside his wife. Her uncle died inside a woman who wasn't his wife. Her dad died inside Mona. Girl had her door closed and earphones in, but she still heard Mona scream. It was different from her usual screams about Girl's too-loud music or the dad's too-much smoking. She didn't sound angry, just scared, and when Girl walked into the bedroom Mona shared with the dad, she found Mona wrapped in a sheet and yelling into a phone. Girl's dad was on the carpet beside the bed, and Girl couldn't tell if Mona had pulled him there or if he had slipped off. She'd never before seen him naked and it was strange to sit down next to him like that, but she did. She pulled his head onto her lap, ran her fingers through his hair and asked him not to leave. That's when Mona stopped yelling and moaned, 'Oh, Mom, oh, Mom,' into the phone. It made Girl wish she could do that, take all the sad she felt and tell it to someone else.

After Girl's dad died, she was sent to live in a youth home. She's been there for two years now and she likes it well enough. What she doesn't like is the logoed minibus that takes the girls in the home to school each day, because it means she has to answer questions from other kids, those who get dropped off in SUVs and sedans or even walk to school because that's how close they live.

'Today we'll start a new book,' Mrs. Adler says. '*The Witch of Blackbird Pond.*' Girl's in the eighth grade and Mrs. Adler is her homeroom teacher. She wears Birkenstocks and silver-turquoise jewelry and makes Girl sit in the front row because she says she needs to keep an eye on her. 'You always look like you're plotting something,' she said once. Girl has tried to tell Mrs. Adler that it wasn't *really* her who pulled the fire alarm last year, or stink-bombed Mr. Ludwig's car, or put fish in one of the sixth-grade lockers, or hid Mr. Ludwig's glasses in one of the toilets right before his big speech on parent assembly night. But Mrs. Adler refuses to listen.

'This looks dumb,' Lien, who sits beside Girl, says as she hands Girl her copy. On the cover is a girl alone in the woods at night, and even though she's looking away so it's impossible to really see her face, to Girl, she doesn't look like much of a witch. Her hair is too pretty and so is her dress. When Girl flips the book over, she's careful to not look at the summary but lets herself read the sentence above it. THERE WAS SOMETHING STRANGE ABOUT AMERICA, SOMETHING THAT THEY ALL SEEMED TO SHARE AND UNDERSTAND AND SHE DID NOT. It makes Girl remember something her dad used to say, about being in the West and how the Arabic word for west was connected to the word strange. Isn't that something? he would ask. Girl now wishes she had asked him what he meant. Isn't west a direction? Doesn't it depend on where you stand?

During lunch, Girl sits with Lien and Marcy and picks at the food on her tray. Each day the cafeteria serves meals from a different culture: Italian, Mexican, Chinese, and American. Girl knows the food is in fact the same soft noodles, that only the sauce changes. Today is Italian and the sauce is red and lumpy and tastes like ketchup. She stands up, carries her tray back to the counter, and hands it to one of the lunch ladies. 'What's wrong with it today?' the lady asks.

'I don't eat pork,' Girl says. The lady shakes her head and dumps the food in the trash.

At the table, Lien and Marcy unwrap homemade turkey sandwiches and open snack-size bags of cheesy chips and chocolate-dipped cookies. Marcy reaches over and hands Girl a few chips. Lien gives her a cookie. She eats them and pretends to not want the other things they offer. As she eats she thinks about her dad, who made fajitas and lasagna and curry, served big portions and ate his quickly. A few times Mona asked why he never made Syrian food and he said he didn't know how, or that it was too hard. Girl could tell Mona didn't believe him. A year before he died Mona looked up recipes and made an entire Syrian dinner. Girl doesn't know what it was because she refused to eat it, but she had sat with them and watched how for the first time her dad ate slowly and carefully, and she couldn't tell if it made him happy or sad.

After lunch Mrs. Adler announces a lesson on World Religions and no one pays attention. Marcy braids Lien's hair and Girl tries to not watch Ryan Delaney flirt with Isabelle Henning. She can see Isabelle's hand in his, and him drawing something on it with a red pen. Ryan always draws things on Isabelle, and Girl wonders if she likes it. She also wonders how long it takes Isabelle to wash it off each night and why she never draws on him. Mrs. Adler shouts Girl's name. A few students laugh and Girl can feel their stares. 'I asked,' Mrs. Adler says, 'if you can tell the class what you know about Mohammed's ascent to heaven?'

Ryan stops marking Isabelle and twists in his seat to face Girl. 'Come on. No one can go all the way to heaven on a horse,' he says. 'How stupid.' More kids laugh, and when Isabelle crosses her arms, Girl sees Ryan's name written across the back of her hand. She feels her face grow hot and when she looks at Ryan chewing on the red pen and looking at her, she knows she's close enough to lean in and shove it straight back into his throat if she wanted to.

'Do you want to disagree with that?' Mrs. Adler says. When Girl shakes her head, Ryan laughs and turns to Isabelle so she laughs too. Mrs. Adler tells them both to be quiet. 'I knew you weren't paying attention,' she says to Girl. Girl feels her face get hotter and she wants to say something but has no idea what, tries to remember anything she's ever heard about a winged horse or a trip to heaven or even Mohammed, but can't.

**

From her dad Girl learned that her grandfather had spent over a decade preparing for priesthood. When he was twelve, his parents had caught him stealing a bottle of arak – booze only better, Girl's dad said. He also said Girl's great-grandparents loved arak and music and parties, and that's how Girl's grandfather began drinking in the first place. But, of course, he couldn't tell his parents what he'd done was their fault, so he blamed it on the devil. Satan himself had tricked him, he swore, and he couldn't be sure it wouldn't happen again. Girl's great-grandparents didn't want their only son to go to hell, or worse, prison, so they sent him away, to a boarding school, then a seminary so he could live a holy life. What about them? Girl asked. They stopped drinking, her dad said, for a while anyway, and sprinkled their house with holy water.

Girl wanted to know why her grandfather didn't just admit he'd lied. It turned out he liked it, the Bible, the stories, all of it. He thought it would be nice to one day become a bishop and wear the red velvet capes and gold tassels and have people bow before him at the altar. But just before he was about to become a priest, Girl's dad said, her grandfather saw the woman he would marry. She wasn't dressed up or trying to catch a man, Girl's dad wanted her to know. No. She was in a housedress and standing just outside her family's courtyard, yelling at a neighbor who'd said something lewd to her younger sister.

In under a week Girl's grandfather left the Church, became a Muslim, and asked to marry the woman who would become Girl's grandmother. Of course, his father had a heart attack and died from the scandal, and his mother disowned him. She saw him just one more time, Girl's dad said, years later, when she was dying. She refused to receive the sacrament of the sick from anyone but him, and he agreed. Girl found that part of the story the saddest, that for so long her great-grandmother probably missed her son but had come to believe it wasn't okay to say so.

**

After school Robert the counselor tells the girls that a group of potential foster parents will visit after dinner. He then pulls Girl aside and asks if she's ready to get serious about being placed. 'Listen, you're both smart and pretty,' he says. 'You look like you could be anybody's kid.'

Girl tries to go around him, but he moves when she moves and blocks her way. She lets him talk for another ten minutes, and then begins to groan. She folds herself in half, falls to the carpet, and groans some more. 'I think I'm getting my period,' she says.

Robert's face turns red, but he does at last move. 'I know what you're doing,' he says, 'and I know that hasn't happened yet. We keep charts of these things.'

Girl is happy when he leaves but she also feels bad for Robert. When his mother died he had brought her what he said were his mother's favorite novels. 'They might be what your mom might've given you if she could,' he'd said. They were mostly romance thriller detective books and Girl didn't like that the women had names like Kendra and Alicia and spent most of their time running toward or away from men named Jake and Eli, but she read them anyway. It seemed to make Robert happy.

After dinner the girls gather in the living room alongside three couples who chat to them in turn and ask them about themselves. In a corner, Robert sits and watches. 'You have beautiful hair,' a woman named Anne tells Girl. 'I could show you how to straighten it.'

Girl looks at Anne's hair, and to her it looks stiff and dry like dead grass. She wants to tell Anne she can show her how to not straighten it, but she knows Robert is watching. 'Great,' she says.

**

Girl's dad liked to say that when he met Girl's mother she had hair like dark woven silk, but in the two photographs Girl has of her mother, her hair grows like a thick shrub. In both pictures she has her head turned away, so Girl can only see half her face. But in each one she's turned a different direction, so if Girl thinks of both photos at once she can nearly see her whole face.

Girl has had the same dream about her mother since she was five. In it the two are climbing a giant tree and Girl struggles to keep up. Each time she reaches her mother, her mother pulls herself even higher, and Girl gets scared she can't keep up, that she's not as strong. Like claws her mother's fingers dig into the bark, and she can pull herself up three or four feet at a time. But Girl's nails are broken and her fingertips are cut. Halfway through the dream she can no longer see her mother and has to climb on alone. At last she reaches the top, exhausted but not scared, her hands covered in dried blood.

Reading in bed before lights out, Girl decides *The Witch of Blackbird Pond* isn't bad as far as school books go. In her book log she writes, *This book is about a girl named Kit who moves from Barbados to America after her grandfather dies. The Puritans in her new village are a bunch of crazies who are suspicious of her because she wears fancy dresses and knows how to swim.* Girl is at the part where everyone gangs up on Kit and accuses her of being a witch, and she wonders if they'll burn her at the stake, or stone her to death.

II

'I'm lactose intolerant,' Girl says, 'and allergic to cats.' It's her first day with her new foster parents, Anne and Mark, and she isn't sure why she's said what she has, only that it has something to do with Anne pacing around the kitchen clutching a drooling gray kitten to her chest and Mark not asking if she liked grilled cheese sandwiches before putting one on her plate.

'Just eat the fries,' Mark says. He gets up and whispers something into Anne's ear, and Anne squeezes the kitten closer. Girl nearly says it's fine, that she can learn to live with Mr. Snickers the cat, but before she can decide if she will or not, Anne leaves the kitchen. 'She'll take him to her mother's,' Mark says.

Girl likes Anne and Mark's house. It reminds her of houses she's seen in magazines, all creams and whites and plenty of carpets, cushions, seascape paintings and real flowers in glass vases. Unlike the rest of the house, her room is filled with color, purple walls and pink bedcovers, and when she and the social worker stood in the room that morning, Girl wondered why everything smelled like paint. 'What color was it before?' she asked.

'The same. We just refreshed it,' Mark said. He hovered in the doorway with Anne, and Girl began to say something about poisonous fumes but noticed Anne's hands clasped together tight enough to turn her knuckles white so she stayed quiet. When the social worker left, Anne helped Girl unpack, and when she found in a drawer a photograph of an older couple surrounded by children, she removed it and apologized. 'These are my parents and all of their grandkids,' she said, and Girl nodded.

**

When Girl's grandfather died it was on top of her grandmother. Girl's dad didn't say this to Girl, but to his friends, the ones who came to play cards and gossip and give Mona a hard time. Girl wasn't allowed in the room while they played, but she snuck near enough to listen to what was said. Many of the stories her dad told she already knew, but she wanted to hear the ones she didn't, and when he told the ones she did know, she wanted to hear how he changed the details.

Girl's dad said that after his father's funeral people swore they could hear his mother speaking to her dead husband as if he were still alive. When Mona asked what it was the grandmother said, Girl wanted to know too. But Girl's dad couldn't answer. 'Didn't you say they were all listening?' Mona asked. Yes, he nodded, 'They were all trying to hear his replies.'

On her tenth birthday Girl's dad gave her a framed photograph of her grandmother. She recognized it as a large copy of the one he carried folded in his wallet. The creases from the original were now thick white lines that slashed across her grandmother's face. 'You look like her. You look like your father's family,' her dad said. Girl shook her head. 'No, I look like my mother,' she said, and as he turned away she thought she saw him nod.

On the television, the image of the news anchor cuts away to footage of people on boats. Girl sits on the sofa with Mark and Anne, and she wonders why the boats, with so many people on them, are blow-up and not the real kind. The image cuts to the people getting off the boats. All of them are wet. Some cry. Some carry children. 'It's a shame,' Mark says.

Girl wants to ask why, and what has happened to these people. 'They're running away, from danger, war,' Anne says, sensing the question. 'Some of them anyway.'

'Will they stay there?' Girl asks. 'On the beach, I mean.'

Mark looks at her and nods. 'Some will, nearby. Some will keep traveling. And some will be sent back, if it's not really dangerous where they're from.'

'Who decides what's dangerous?' Girl asks. Anne shrugs and so does Mark.

On the screen, a woman with a baby bends down and touches her forehead to the wet sand, kisses the ground, then the baby, and again the ground. Then she sits with the hand not holding the baby open, so her palm faces the sky, and her lips move.

'The poor thing has lost her mind,' Mark says as the same woman again touches her head to the ground, over and over, the baby still in her arms.

'She's praying,' Girl says. 'My dad prayed like that.'

'Oh,' Mark says, and turns to her. 'We didn't know that. That's fine, of course.' He clears his throat and smiles, then looks at Anne.

'Of course, it's fine,' Anne says, also smiling. For a moment no one speaks, then Mark changes the channel. 'Just know,' Anne says, 'that in this house, you can do what you like, and wear what you like,' and her smile reminds Girl of the smile Robert would make when he was worried about one of the girls embarrassing him, or getting him into trouble, and she asks to go to bed.

Girl's grandfather became a real Muslim, Girl's dad liked to say, but he still named his three eldest sons, Samuel, Sammy, and Sam, after his father. Imagine what people thought, Girl's dad said, three Muslim boys with names from the Bible! Girl didn't understand. What's the big deal? she asked, and he looked at her like it was the most obvious thing in the world. By the time Girl's father, the fourth son, was born, Girl's great-grandmother was dead, and there was no one left to make proud or upset, and Girl's grandfather gave his youngest son, her dad, a Muslim name instead. And that's the difference between my brothers and me, Girl's dad said.

When Girl asked her dad about her uncles he shrugged or changed the subject. If he did speak of them, it was to tell her funny things from when he was young, and they were young, and long before Girl was born. If she wanted to know anything else, like where they were now, and why they never visited or even called, he closed his eyes instead of answering. To Girl, it looked like he was reaching down, all the way inside himself. Each time she hoped he would find something new, and each time he opened his eyes and told her another story, from long ago and far away, and she stopped asking.

**

In the passenger seat Anne's entire body shakes but she does not speak. The one time she inhales deeply enough to make Girl think she might say something, Mark's hand reaches out from the steering wheel and holds hers still. In the backseat, Girl wears a scarf, not around her neck, but over her hair and tied beneath her chin. She has her earphones in but keeps the volume turned low in case they say something, but they don't. Looking at herself in the rearview mirror she thinks that with the scarf she does after all look like her grandmother, at least a little.

In class, Mrs. Adler stops speaking mid-sentence and looks at her. She starts to say something, and stops again, and assigns the class quiet reading time instead. Marcy leans over and tells Girl she wishes she could wear a scarf over her hair too. 'So dumbass people would stop asking to touch my braids,' she says. Mrs. Adler shushes them both and tells them to take out their books.

Girl reads about Kit getting used to the colony: she teaches Sunday school classes even though she thinks church is boring, and she even gets engaged to a rich guy named William, who all the girls want to marry. But then she tries to make the Sunday school fun and has the kids act out a story from the Bible and Girl can tell all hell will break loose, and it does. The school shuts down and Kit escapes into the woods. There, she meets a woman named Hannah who's not allowed in the colony because she's a Quaker. Girl knows the best thing Kit can do now is stay in the woods with Hannah, but she also knows Kit won't.

During lunch kids nudge one another and stare at Girl as she walks through the cafeteria. Marcy sticks out her tongue at some of them until they look away and Lien flips off a few until it makes Marcy and Girl laugh. No one looks as much as the kids at Ryan's table and in the corner of her eye Girl sees Isabelle. She thinks of how, when they were younger, Isabelle's mom would drive the two of them to school and Girl's dad would pick them up and take them to the park or for ice cream. She remembers the sleepovers, and trips to the pool, and how they held hands everywhere they went.

At the counter, one of the lunch ladies shakes her head at Girl when she sees her. 'What's that on your head?' she asks.

'A kind of experiment,' Girl says. The lady nods, like she understands, and when Girl asks for two chocolate milks, she gives them to her.

When Girl reaches Ryan's table they don't immediately notice her, and when they do, Isabelle's eyes grow big and she looks away. 'Do you want some chocolate milk?' Girl asks her.

'Go away, loser,' Ryan says.

'Do you?' she asks again.

'I said, go away, Osama,' Ryan says, and his friends laugh with him.

'Just leave the milk and go,' Isabelle says.

'Did you know my dad died?' Girl whispers. Isabelle's eyes turn sad, and Girl wants to say, It's okay, I'm fine, It just hurts to swallow. 'Why do you hang out with them?' she says instead. Girl watches Isabelle's eyes change back.

'They're not that bad,' Isabelle says. 'Anyway, you're the one making a scene.' Someone else at the table says something that makes the others laugh, and Girl walks away.

Back at her table Girl shakes her head at the sandwich Lien holds, but Lien puts it down in front of her anyway. 'What were you even doing over there?' Lien asks.

'I felt bad for her. She always looks miserable hanging out with them.'

Lien rolls her eyes. 'Girl,' Marcy says, 'she's exactly where she wants to be.' Girl thinks Marcy might be right, but that there's still something about it that's not, though she doesn't know what it is.

'I'll be back,' she says, standing up.

At Ryan's table again, she feels her face get hot and she tells herself to walk away, to go back to her own table. But she knows that already it's too late, and before they speak or laugh, she smacks the milk carton down on the table and watches the cardboard break. Ryan screams and jumps straight up, but he's too slow. Chocolate splatters onto his arms and turns parts of his white t-shirt brown. His friends begin to yell, and Girl knows she'll be sent to the principal's office and begins to head there herself. When she reaches the cafeteria doors, she looks back one last time and sees Isabelle helping Ryan clean himself up.

Mark picks Girl up after school and tells her he has good news and bad news. 'Seems your uncle is looking for you,' he says.

'He's dead!' Girl says, then remembers there are still two others.

Mark laughs. 'He sounded pretty alive to me. Listen, he wants to get to know you better, to become your legal guardian, have you live with him and his family.'

Girl tries to understand but can't. 'I don't even know him,' she says. She looks at Mark, but he stares ahead at the road, and she wishes he would turn and look at her.

'Don't worry. They agreed to let you stay with us the rest of the school year. Everyone thinks that's for the best. But they're asking to fly you out to Milwaukee this weekend.'

Girl wants to ask Mark if he spoke to her uncle himself, what he sounded like, if he said why he'd never visited, if Mark thought he'd like her. 'So what's the bad news?' she asks instead.

'I'll be sad to see you leave,' he says. 'I was hoping you'd be with us longer.'

Girl feels her chest grow tight. Through the window, she can see a small bird in a tree extend its wings like it might fly. Instead it draws them in again, the brightest feathers disappearing underneath the darker ones on top, and hops from one branch to the next.

**

When Girl's uncle Samuel died, he was with his mistress, not his wife. This is a story Girl heard her dad tell Mona. They had come back late from dinner and she was on the sofa pretending to be asleep. She could hear them in the kitchen as he crushed ice and poured drinks, and when they walked into the living room she stayed quiet and hoped he wouldn't send her to bed. When Mona told him to wake her, he sat on the rug instead and asked Mona to sit beside him.

Girl learned that Samuel had mixed Viagra and cholesterol pills for what her dad said was a good time, and that the mistress was in fact a prostitute. Girl's dad also said that when the mistress slipped out from under Girl's uncle she smoked a cigarette before she called for help. After Samuel died, his wife took their only daughter and moved to Vienna where her sister lived. But she did this only after finding the mistress. Girl's dad said the wife and the mistress talked for hours, all night and through the next day. When Mona asked how he knew that, he said, 'Everybody knew!' They even kept in touch, he said. Long-distance phone calls and letters pages long. It became a scandal, he said. But when Mona asked what was in the letters, he didn't know. Girl lay on the sofa trying to keep still and also wanting the answer. Why had no one asked the women what they were writing, she wanted to know, what it was they said?

III

At the airport in Milwaukee, Girl is greeted by a man with a goatee and two identically dressed girls who look about five and seven. He holds a sign with Girl's name spelled out, first and last, and she cringes as people connect her to it and the man. When he sees her, he flings the sign aside to hug her, and tells his daughters to do the same. He leans in and hugs them all, too close and too tight and Girl can't breathe.

In the car the little girls scream in the backseat and Girl's uncle speaks loudly over them both, but Girl doesn't listen. She thinks only about how he looks like her dad, his goatee and its bits of gray, eyes that squint in the light. His nose flares when he inhales and when he says *there* it sounds like *zere*. She rolls down the window and rests her head against the door, lets the cold air hit her face as they move. 'Are you okay?' he asks, and she says Yes.

Girl thinks about what happens when someone has a heart attack. How the main artery becomes too blocked to allow oxygen to pass. That without oxygen, the muscle cells and tissues begin to die. She knows that sometimes a person can survive an attack. The muscle can heal like a skin wound, and like a wound, a scar forms over the damage. But after that, the heart just isn't as strong. It can't beat as hard, or as much. She also knows that sometimes a person can't survive at all, and in that case, the heart just starves to death.

They spend half the day in the mall and the other half in front of the TV watching a movie with talking animals. Girl's uncle laughs the loudest when a pig farts or a bird flies into a tree, and halfway through the movie, Girl's aunt asks if Girl would like to look at photo albums instead.

Upstairs, the two of them sit on the bedroom carpet and the aunt lets Girl turn the pages. Most of the photos are of her uncle as a young man and of her aunt and uncle at their wedding. But toward the end of the album are a few with faded color or no color at all, and her aunt touches one of four boys standing in a line, their arms wrapped around one another, their smiles identical. 'There,' she says, and points to the boy on the end, the one holding a ball and looking at the camera.

Girl looks at the boy who's also her dad and wonders what he felt like when the photo was taken. She knows he must have been hot because his face is shiny, that he must have been playing, running and sweating, when he was told to stop and stand still. His smile is wide and everywhere on his face, in his round cheeks and eyes. The alley behind the boys is mostly covered by their bodies, but she wants to know what it looks like, what it all looked like, so that maybe then she'd know how he felt. 'Do you think he was sad he never went back?' she asks.

'It's hard to know,' her aunt says. 'Do you think he was?'

Girl shrugs and flips back a few pages and points to one photo of a priest holding a baby, and then another. 'Your cousins' baptisms,' her aunt says. Girl tries to not look confused, but she is, and she can tell her aunt knows, so she waits. 'Listen,' her aunt says. 'Your grandfather was Christian. That made your uncle Christian. It made your father Christian. Do you understand? It passes through the father. It doesn't matter who converted and who named who what.' Girl does understand. She understands this is why her father and uncle didn't speak. But what about my mother? she wants to ask. What did she believe? But she senses that her aunt, even if she knows, will not tell. 'Tomorrow we're taking you to church,' her aunt says. 'You might like it.'

In church, the service is in Arabic and Girl understands nothing. Robed men and boys walk up and down the aisles, some of them slowly swinging chains attached to silver balls filled with smoke, and everyone looks tired.

When the service ends and people rise to leave, Girl does too. 'Wait,' her uncle says. He loops his arm through hers and leads her to the back of the church, to a room with rows of chairs, a chalkboard and a group of kids half her age. He says something in Arabic to the only adult in the room – a man wearing glasses and itchy-looking wool – smiles at her and leaves. Girl is thinking about what it would feel like to follow him out, to scream and yell in the middle of that church, when a kid her age walks in. He tells her his name is Danny and that he's fourteen. He also says he'd rather be shooting his BB gun, watching football or kissing girls. 'My mom just found God though,' he says.

'Where was he hiding?' Girl asks.

'Everyone, be quiet, please,' the man with the glasses says, then he opens a book and starts reading from it in Arabic. Girl looks up at the clock and calculates the hours until her flight. She thinks about the next day and school, about Mark and Anne, Lien and Marcy, Ryan and Isabelle, Mrs. Adler. About her dad, her grandfather and her uncles, her grandmother and her mother. Always her thoughts lead to her mother.

**

Girl's dad was married to Mona when he met Girl's mom. He was from Damascus and Girl's mom was from Latakia, they met in Las Vegas, and she died soon after Girl was born. These are the things Girl knows. Each time she asked her dad for more he told her only stories about Damascus, her grandparents and uncles, other people she did not know. Many times, she tried to imagine what it was like when Mona found out, what it looked like when Girl's dad came home with a baby in his arms. For a while, Girl wondered if at the beginning Mona had spoiled her, dressed her in skirts and bonnets and pushed her around the neighborhood in a stroller, if she had told people that Girl was, of course, her daughter. But Girl now knows that these things could not have happened. Because later, when Girl was older, many times she heard Mona tell Girl's dad she would never forgive him. She would say it even if she saw Girl nearby, even if she knew she could hear her.

When Girl's dad died, Mona at last decided that Girl definitely was not her daughter. A social worker asked if Girl had family but neither Mona nor Girl knew where the uncles were, or if they were even still alive. All Girl could do was show the social worker the two photos of her mother and explain how thinking about both at once would make it easier to see the full face, to know what her mother really looked like. The social worker tried to reason with Mona, told her thoughts like hers were normal and that they soon would pass. But Girl knew they wouldn't, because Mona continued to look at her the same way she'd always looked at her, like she was something heavy, that like plaque she would one day kill her heart too.

**

When Danny asks Girl if she wants to kiss she thinks about it and says 'Yes.' The two are alone in the rector's office, waiting to be picked up, and he moves his chair closer to hers and leans over. Girl likes that his lips feel soft but his breath smells like onion rings and he's not very good at moving his tongue. He pushes it into her mouth and shoves it against her cheeks and toward her throat, and she pulls away. 'You're making it hard to breathe,' she says.

'Sorry. Can I try again?' She feels bad for him and says 'Sure' and this time it's not much better and again she starts to pull away when the rector's assistant walks in. He yells at them in Arabic until his face is bright red and they try to not laugh. Girl feels bad for him and tries to interrupt. 'We don't know what you're saying,' she says, but the assistant doesn't hear or listen.

On the way to the airport Girl's uncle speaks only to quote the Bible and her aunt sits in the backseat, covering the kids' ears. When they near the terminal, the aunt's hand reaches from behind the passenger seat where Girl sits and squeezes her shoulder, and Girl wants to say she would like to stay, that she'll go to any church or masjid, pagoda or fire temple, if they keep her. But the moment passes, and the aunt takes her hand back, and the uncle's voice again fills the car. 'Do you not know that your bodies are members of Christ? Shall I then take the members of Christ and make them members of a prostitute? Never!'

On the plane a man asks to switch seats with Girl so he can sit next to his son. Girl turns to the seat he points to beside her and thinks about moving, but the kid looks nine or ten and he's watching his iPad. He doesn't care where his dad sits. When she says 'No' the man looks surprised and asks again, and this time, his question doesn't sound like one. She wants to tell him she has to sit next to the window, that if she doesn't her chest will get tight for no reason at all, that it'll be his fault if she has a heart attack right there on the plane in the middle of the flight. Even a child's heart can stop, she wants to say. But then the boy looks up at his dad and then at her, and their stares make it hard to think, so she gets up and lets them have it. 'Thank you,' they both say, but she pretends not to hear, sits in her new seat, takes out her book and reads.

In *The Witch of Blackbird Pond* a bad illness kills off a lot of Puritans and it gets Kit in trouble. Girl is annoyed that even though Kit has nothing to do with the disease, she's still blamed for it. But so many people are dying, and no one knows why, and they've spent so much time thinking about Kit and her dresses and how she can swim, and it all suddenly makes sense to them that she's a witch and the reason behind all of their problems. Girl doesn't like Kit enough to be sad if they kill her. But she wants someone to at least say, Listen, this is crazy, sure Kit wears fancy dresses and acts stuck-up and spends all of her time hanging out with a boring Quaker woman, but that doesn't mean anything.

In the baggage claim Girl expects to see Mark but instead it's Anne and she looks nervous. Her hair is uncombed, and her eyes can't focus. On the freeway she drives slowly and when a car honks, she doesn't seem to notice. They don't speak at all and when they've nearly reached the house Anne turns to Girl and tries to smile. 'I'm glad you reunited with your family,' she says.

Girl nods so she doesn't have to answer, and when they pull into the garage, and the door comes down, she says, 'Why don't you and Mark have children?' For a while Anne sits and doesn't answer, then she begins to cry. Girl wants to say she's sorry, but it's dark inside the car and the porch light coming in through the garage window shadows Anne's face, and Girl pretends it's her mother's.

In class the next day Mrs. Adler continues the discussion on World Religions and Girl does her best to pay attention. 'Next up: Buddhism,' Mrs. Adler says. 'Lien, why don't you tell us what you know about the dharma?' The entire class turns to look at Lien. Marcy gives Girl a look to say, Here we go. Girl is tired and has felt sick all morning. Mrs. Adler's voice scratches at her ears, and she feels her body grow hot.

'So, we each have a body and a spirit, and the spirit can live in the body or not,' Lien says. 'And what happens to your spirit depends on your karma. Like if you help people you have good karma, but if you've been a big B, your karma's definitely bad.' A few kids laugh but Mrs. Adler nods along. Girl wonders if she's even listening. Lien takes a deep breath to go again, and Girl feels her gut twist like someone is wringing it out. 'And the nirvana is connected to the dharma, because if your dharma is good then you can reach nirvana,' Lien says.

When Girl raises her hand, Lien stops speaking and Mrs. Adler looks at Girl but doesn't call on her. 'Go ahead, Lien,' she says. But Lien doesn't, and instead looks at Girl and nods.

'She's just saying words,' Girl says. 'Her mom's Jewish, her dad's an atheist, and she believes in UFOs. All that stuff is from an anime, about Jesus Christ and Buddha living together in an apartment in Japan.'

'It's a really good anime,' Marcy says.

'Girls!' Mrs. Adler yells.

'Also, Kit is a hypocrite,' Girl says. She's hot and dizzy and she doesn't care what Mrs. Adler might do to her as long as she gets to speak. 'I've been thinking about it. At the beginning of the book she's sad because she has to leave her fancy plantation and live without slaves, and by the end of the book she's learned that slavery is bad but she still calls Indians savages and I'm pretty sure she'd kill one if she had to, the same way the villagers wanted to kill her.'

'What the hell?' Lien says. 'She can't have slaves. She's from Barbados. Marcy's dad is from Barbados.'

'Um, hello. She's white,' Marcy says.

'I didn't know there were white people in Barbados,' Lien says.

'Okay, enough!' Mrs. Adler says. She points at Girl, then the door. 'Principal's office.'

Sweat soaks the pits of Girl's shirt and her stomach hurts, and the principal has five students to see before it's her turn. She's told to sit in the waiting area next to the nurse's office and when she asks the nurse if she can use the bathroom he tells her to stay put where she is. It's only when she threatens to puke right there, on desks and chairs and floor, that he hands her the key.

Leaning over the toilet, she tries to throw up but can't. All she wants is to lie down somewhere cool and quiet and without people. She pulls her pants down and sits but nothing happens, and the pain travels through her body in waves. It's then she looks down and sees the blood fall one drop at a time and dissolve in the water. The waves grow stronger, crash against her insides, and she watches the blood drop more quickly until the drops connect and form a stream and she reaches out and touches it. It's thicker than regular blood and sticks to her hand like glue. 'You need to come out now,' the nurse shouts through the door. Girl closes her eyes and tries to reach down, all the way down, past her dad's voice and stories, to what he's left out, the places between his words. To why Mona had to hate her and why her mother had to die, to why the men in her family died inside women, and why, when they did, it was the women who disappeared. She opens her eyes and stays there, sitting, as the nurse knocks, then pounds on the door. She thinks about cleaning herself up and asking to go home, about who will pick her up and where they'll take her, about the kind of pain that comes with blood and the kind that doesn't. She wipes her fingers and watches the blood dry on the toilet paper. This can be anyone's, she thinks, not just mine or my mother's. It could be Anne's or Mrs. Adler's. My aunt's and grandmother's. Mona's even. She folds a long strip of toilet paper and holds it between her legs, pulls up her pants, and washes her hands.

When she opens the door, the nurse stands in her way. He's tall and heavy and his body fills the doorway. But she doesn't care what he's saying. She ignores his words and pushes her way through. 'Shut up already,' she says, and when she looks back, his face is red and his eyes surprised, and she doesn't feel bad for him. She feels good. She feels okay.

Acknowledgments

This book was made possible by those who champion the short story and have supported my writing over the years. Thank you to the Bridport Prize, Bristol Short Story Prize, Northern Writers Awards, Enizagam Literary Awards, Society of Authors' Awards and Deborah Rogers Foundation. Thank you to Kwame Dawes for valuable edits on "In the Land of Kan'an." Thank you to Lancaster University. To Jenn Ashworth, whose feedback and insights led to important edits. To Robert Alan Jamieson and Alice Thompson, who told me to keep writing.

Thank you to my U.S. editors Eric Obenauf and Eliza Wood-Obenauf at Two Dollar Radio for being dream collaborators. To my U.K. editor Ansa Khan at Picador for careful, thoughtful edits. To my agent Juliet Pickering for finding and guiding me, as well as to Samuel Hodder and everyone at Blake Friedmann. To Kim Witherspoon and Maria Whelan at Inkwell. To Dr. Sarah Gualtieri, whose brilliant and necessary research in *Between Arab and White* directly inspired and informed the title story in this book.

I am thankful, especially, to the women who have told me stories, and listened to mine: Rosie, Cait, Janelle and Jaclyn. To my nieces, Lola and Alana. To my siblings. And to my mother and grandmother, who helped me realize the stories we still need to tell.

A special thank-you to the O'Gormans for their kindness and support. And to Alan, who makes the tea, and helped me find home.

Some of the stories in this book previously appeared in the following: "In the Land of Kan'an" in *Prairie Schooner*; "Summer of the Shark" in *Enizagam*; "Disappearance" in *Bridport Prize Anthology*; and "Ghusl" in *Bristol Short Story Prize Anthology*.